THE TRAIN

GEORGES SIMENON (1903–1989) was born in Liège, Belgium, the son of an accountant. His father's ill health forced him to quit school at 16, and he became a newspaperman, assigned to the crime beat. He published his first book, *Au Point des arches,* a year later, under his reporter's pen-name, G. Sim. In 1922 he moved to Paris and began to write novels at a furious pace, using at least a dozen pen-names, although he created his most famous character, Commissaire Maigret of the Paris Police, under his own name. Maigret would eventually star in 75 novels. His non-Maigret novels—referred to as his *roman durs* (literally, "hard novels")—were even more critically acclaimed, leading to speculation he would eventually win the Nobel. In the early thirties Simenon took up travel, living on a houseboat cruising the Belgian canal system, touring Africa and the Soviet Union, and living throughout the US and Canada. During the war years he moved to the French countryside, but was harassed by the Nazis who suspected his last name was Jewish. Nonetheless, after the war he was banned from publishing for five years for having sold film rights to German filmmakers. Married and divorced twice, Simenon was the father of four children, one of whom, his daughter Mari-Jo, committed suicide at age 25. (She would be the subject of his novel, *The Disappearance of Odile.*) It would darken Simenon's later years, but he never stopped writing. Estimates are that he wrote as many as 500 books by the time of his death of natural causes at age 86.

ROBERT BALDICK (1927–1972) was a British author and translator, in addition to being a Fellow at Pembroke College, Oxford and joint editor of the Penguins Classics series.

THE NEVERSINK LIBRARY

I was by no means the only reader of books on board the Neversink. Several other sailors were diligent readers, though their studies did not lie in the way of belles-lettres. Their favourite authors were such as you may find at the book-stalls around Fulton Market; they were slightly physiological in their nature. My book experiences on board of the frigate proved an example of a fact which every booklover must have experienced before me, namely, that though public libraries have an imposing air, and doubtless contain invaluable volumes, yet, somehow, the books that prove most agreeable, grateful, and companionable, are those we pick up by chance here and there; those which seem put into our hands by Providence; those which pretend to little, but abound in much. —HERMAN MELVILLE, *WHITE JACKET*

THE TRAIN

GEORGES SIMENON

TRANSLATED BY ROBERT BALDICK

MELVILLE HOUSE PUBLISHING
BROOKLYN, NEW YORK

THE TRAIN

Originally published in French as *Le Train*

The Train © 1958 Georges Simenon Limited,
a Chorion company. All rights reserved

Translated by Robert Baldick
Translation © Penguin Books, Ltd.

First Melville House printing: May 2011

Melville House Publishing
145 Plymouth Street
Brooklyn, NY 11201

www.mhpbooks.com

ISBN: 978-1-935554-46-2

Printed in the United States of America
 2 3 4 5 6 7 8 9 10

   Library of Congress Cataloging-in-Publication Data

Simenon, Georges, 1903-1989.
 [Train. English]
 The train / Georges Simenon ; translated from the French by Robert
Baldick.
    p. cm.
 Originally published in French as Le Train.
 ISBN 978-1-935554-46-2
 1. World War, 1939-1945--Refugees--Belgium--Fiction. 2. Jewish women-
-Fiction. I. Baldick, Robert. II. Title.
 PQ2637.I53T6613 2011
 843'.912--dc22

                    2011018460

THE TRAIN

1

WHEN I WOKE UP, A YELLOWISH LIGHT WHICH
I knew so well was filtering into the bedroom through the
holland curtains. Our windows, on the first floor, have no
shutters. None of the houses in the street has any. I could
hear, on the bedside table, the ticking of the alarm clock,
and, beside me, my wife's regular breathing, which was almost as loud as that of patients, at the movies, during an
operation. She was then seven and a half months pregnant.
As when she was expecting Sophie, her huge belly forced
her to sleep on her back.

Without looking at the alarm clock, I slipped one leg out
of bed. Jeanne stirred and stammered in a faraway voice:

"What time is it?"

"Half past five."

I have always got up early, especially after my years in
the sanatorium, where, in summer, they used to bring us the
thermometer at six in the morning.

My wife had already ceased to be aware of what was
happening around her and one of her arms had stretched
out across the place I had just left.

I dressed silently, carrying out, in order, the ritual movements of every morning, and glancing now and then at my
daughter, whose bed at that time was still in our room. Yet

we had furnished the prettiest room in the house for her, a front room communicating with ours.

She refused to sleep in it.

I went out of the room carrying my slippers in one hand, and put them on only at the foot of the stairs. It was then that I heard the first boats' hooters over at Uf Lock, which is about two miles away. The regulations state that the locks must be open to barge traffic at sunrise, and every morning there is the same concert.

In the kitchen I lit the gas and put the water on to boil. Once again, it looked like being a hot, sunny day. During the whole of that period, we had nothing but glorious days and even now I could still point out, hour by hour, the position of the pools of sunlight in the various rooms in the house.

I opened the back door to the glass porch which we had put on so that my wife can do the washing there in all weathers and my daughter can play there. I can picture the doll's pram, and the doll a little farther off, on the yellow tiles.

I avoided going straight into my workshop because I wanted to obey the rules, as I used to say at that time when speaking of my timetable. A timetable which had established itself, little by little, made up of habits rather than obligations.

While the water was warming up, I poured some corn into an old blue enamel pan with a rusty bottom, which could no longer be used for anything else, and crossed the garden to go and feed the hens. We had six white hens and one cock.

The dew was sparkling on the vegetables and on our solitary lilac, whose flowers, which were early that year, were beginning to wither, and I could still hear, not only the hooting of the boats on the Meuse, but also the panting of the diesel engines.

I want to make it clear right away that I was not an unhappy man, nor a sad man either. At the age of thirty-two, I considered that I had gone beyond all the plans I had made, all my dreams.

I had a wife, a house, and a four-year-old daughter who was rather high-strung, but Dr. Wilhems said that that would pass.

I had a business of my own and my clientele grew from day to day, especially in the last few months of course. Because of what had been happening, everybody wanted to have a radio. I never stopped selling new radios and repairing old ones, and since we lived close to the quayside where the boats stopped for the night, I had the bargees as customers.

I remember that I heard the door open in the house on the left, where the Matrays, a quiet old couple, lived. Monsieur Matray, who worked as a cashier in the Bank of France for thirty-five or forty years, is another early riser and starts every day by going into his garden for a breather.

All the gardens in the street look the same, each as wide as the house and separated from one another by walls just so high that you can see nothing but the top of your neighbor's head.

For some time past, old Monsieur Matray had got into the habit of watching out for me, on account of my sets which could pick up short waves.

"No news this morning, Monsieur Féron."

That day, I went back inside before he asked me the question and I poured the boiling water onto the coffee. The familiar objects were in their places, those that Jeanne and I had allotted them or which they had ended up by taking, almost of their own accord, with the passing of time.

If my wife had not been pregnant, I would have begun to hear her footsteps on the first floor, for she normally got up straight after me. All the same I insisted, out of habit, on making myself my first cup of coffee before going into my workshop. We observed a certain number of rites of that sort, and I suppose the same is true of every family.

The first pregnancy had been painful, the delivery difficult. Jeanne attributed Sophie's nervous temperament to the forceps which had had to be used and which had bruised the child's head. Ever since her second pregnancy had started, she had been dreading a troublesome delivery and she was haunted by the idea of giving birth to an abnormal child.

Dr. Wilhems, in whom she had absolute confidence, could not manage to reassure her, except for a few hours at a time, and at night she found it impossible to fall asleep. Long after we had gone to bed, I could hear her trying to find a comfortable position and she nearly always ended up by asking in a whisper:

"Are you asleep, Marcel?"

"No."

"I wonder if I'm suffering from a deficiency of iron. I've read in an article..."

She tried to drop off to sleep, but often it was two o'clock in the morning before she succeeded and afterward it was not uncommon for her to sit up with a cry.

"I've had another nightmare, Marcel."

"Tell me about it."

"No, I'd rather forget about it. It's too horrible. Forgive

me for stopping you from sleeping, and when you work so hard too…"

Recently she had been getting up about seven o'clock and coming downstairs after that to make breakfast.

With my cup of coffee in one hand, I went into my workshop and opened the glass door which looked out onto the yard and the garden. I was entitled, at that moment, to the first ray of sunshine of the day, a little to the left of the door, and I knew exactly when it would reach my bench.

It isn't a real bench, but a big, heavy table which came from a convent and which I bought at a sale. There are always two or three sets on it which are in the process of being repaired. My tools, arranged in a rack on the wall, are within easy reach. All round the room the deal shelves I had put up were littered with sets, each of which bore the customer's name on a label.

I ended up of course by turning the knobs. It was almost a game with me to put off that moment. I used to tell myself in defiance of all the laws of logic:

"If I wait a little longer, it may be today…"

Straightaway, that particular morning, I realized that something was happening at last. I had never known the air so crowded. Whatever wavelength I picked, broadcasts were overlapping, voices, whistles, phrases in German, Dutch, English, and you could feel a sort of dramatic throbbing in the air.

"During the night, the German armies launched a massive attack on…"

So far it was not France but Holland which had just been invaded. What I could hear was a Belgian station. I tried to get Paris but Paris remained silent.

The patch of sunshine was trembling on the gray floor,

and at the bottom of the garden our six hens were fussing around the cock Sophie called Nestor. Why did I wonder all of a sudden what was going to become of our little poultry yard? I was almost moved to tears by its fate.

I turned some more knobs, searching the short waves where everybody seemed to be talking at once. In that way I picked up, for a brief moment, a military band which I promptly lost, so that I have never known to what army it belonged.

An Englishman was reading a message I could not understand, repeating each sentence as if he were dictating it to a correspondent, and after that I came across a station I had never heard before, a field transmitter.

It was obviously very close, and belonged to one of the regiments which, since October, since the beginning of the phony war, had been camping in the region.

The voices of the two men were as clear as if they had been talking to me on the telephone, and I supposed that they were in the neighborhood of Givet. Not that it matters in the slightest.

"Where is your colonel?"

That one had a strong southern accent.

"All I know is that he isn't here."

"He ought to be."

"What do you want me to do about it?"

"You've got to find him. He sleeps somewhere, doesn't he?"

"I suppose so, but not in his bed."

"In whose bed, then?"

A dirty laugh.

"Here one night, there the next."

Some atmospherics prevented me from hearing the rest,

and I caught sight of Monsieur Matray's white hair and pink face over the wall, at the place where he had installed an old packing case to serve as a stepladder.

"Any news, Monsieur Féron?"

"The Germans have invaded Holland."

"Is that official?"

"The Belgians have announced it."

"And Paris?"

"Paris is playing music."

I heard him dash indoors shouting:

"Germaine! Germaine! This is it! They've attacked!"

I too was thinking that this was it, but the words had a different meaning for me than for Monsieur Matray. I am rather ashamed of saying this, but I felt relieved. I even wonder whether ever since October, indeed ever since Munich, I had not been waiting impatiently for this moment, whether I had not been disappointed every morning, when I turned the knobs of the radio, to learn that the armies were still facing each other without fighting.

It was the 10th of May. A Friday, I am almost sure of that. A month earlier, at the beginning of April, the 8th or 9th, my hopes had risen when the Germans had invaded Denmark and Norway.

I don't know how to explain myself and I wonder if there is anybody capable of understanding me. It will be pointed out that I was in no danger, as, on account of my shortsightedness, I was exempt from military service. My prescription is sixteen diopters, which means that, without my glasses, I am as helpless as somebody in total darkness, or at least in a thick fog.

I have always been terrified of finding myself without my glasses, for example of falling down in the street and breaking them, and I always have a spare pair in my pocket. That's to say nothing of my health, of the four years I spent in a sanatorium, between the ages of fourteen and eighteen, of the check-ups I had to undergo until a few years ago. None of that has anything to do with the impatience I am trying to describe.

I had little hope, at first, of leading a normal life, still less of getting a decent job and starting a family.

Yet I had become a happy man, I want to make that perfectly clear. I loved my wife. I loved my daughter. I loved my house, my habits, and even my street, which, quiet and sunny, ran down to the Meuse.

The fact remains that on the day war was declared I felt a sense of relief. I found myself saying out loud:

"It was bound to happen."

My wife looked at me in astonishment.

"Why?"

"I don't know. I felt certain about it, that's all."

It wasn't France and Germany, or Poland, England, Hitler, Nazism, or Communism which, to my mind, were involved. I have never taken any interest in politics and I don't know anything about it. It would have been as much as I could do to quote the names of three or four French Ministers from having heard them on the radio.

No. This war, which had suddenly broken out after a year of spurious calm, was a personal matter between Fate and me.

I had already experienced one war, in the same town, Fumay, when I was a child, for I was six years old in 1914. I saw my father go off, in uniform, one morning when the rain was pouring down, and my mother was red-eyed all day. I heard the sound of gunfire for nearly four years, especially when we went up in the hills. I remember the Germans and their pointed helmets, the officers' capes, the posters on the walls, rationing, the poor bread, the shortage of sugar, butter, and potatoes.

One November evening I saw my mother come home naked, her hair cropped short, screaming insults and foul words at some youths who were trooping after her.

I was ten years old. We lived in the center of the town, in a first-floor flat.

She dressed without taking any notice of me, a mad look in her eyes, still muttering words I had never heard her use before, and suddenly, ready to go out, with a shawl around her head, she seemed to remember that I was there.

"Madame Jamais will look after you until your father comes home."

Madame Jamais was our landlady and lived on the ground floor. I was too terrified to cry. She didn't kiss me. At the door she hesitated, then she went out without saying anything else and the street door slammed.

I am not trying to explain. I mean that all this may have nothing to do with my feelings in 1939 or 1940. I am putting down the facts as they came back to me, without any falsification.

I contracted tuberculosis four years later. I had two or three other illnesses one after another.

Altogether, my impression, when war broke out, was that Fate was playing another trick on me and I was not surprised for I was practically certain that that was going to happen one day.

This time it wasn't a microbe, a virus, a congenital deformity of heaven knows what part of the eye—the doctors have never been able to agree about my eyes. It was a war which was hurling men against one another in tens of millions.

The idea was ridiculous, I realize that. But the fact remains that I knew, that I was ready. And that waiting, ever since October, was becoming unbearable. I didn't understand. I kept wondering why what was bound to happen didn't happen.

Were they going to tell us, one fine morning, as at Munich, that everything had been settled, that life was going back to normal, that this great panic had just been a mistake?

Wouldn't such a turn of events have meant that something had gone wrong with my personal destiny?

The sunshine was growing warmer, invading the yard, falling on the doll. Our bedroom window opened and my wife called out:

"Marcel!"

I stood up, went out of the workshop, and leaned my head back. My wife looked as if she were wearing a mask, as she had during her first pregnancy. Her face, with the skin all taut, struck me as touching but almost unfamiliar.

"What's happening?"

"You heard?"

"Yes. Is it true? Are they attacking?"

"They've invaded Holland."

And my daughter, behind her, asked:

"What is it, Mummy?"

"Lie down. It isn't time to get up."

"What did Daddy say?"

"Nothing. Go to sleep."

She came down almost at once, smelling of the bed and walking with her legs slightly apart, because of her belly.

"Do you think they'll let them get through?"

"I haven't the faintest idea."

"What does the government say?"

"It hasn't said anything yet."

"What do you intend to do, Marcel?"

"I haven't thought about it. I'm going to try to get some more news."

It was still from Belgium that it was coming, given out by a dramatic staccato voice. This voice announced that at one o'clock in the morning some Messerschmitts and Stukas had flown over Belgian territory and had dropped bombs at several points.

Panzers had entered the Ardennes, and the Belgian government had addressed a solemn appeal to France to help it in its defense.

The Dutch, for their part, were opening their dykes and flooding a large part of the country, and there was talk, if the worst came to the worst, of halting the invader in front of the Albert Canal.

In the meantime my wife was making breakfast and setting the table, and I could hear the clatter of crockery.

"Any more news?"

"Tanks are crossing the Belgian frontier pretty well everywhere."

"But in that case…"

For certain moments of the day, my memories are so precise that I could write a detailed account of them, whereas for others I remember above all else the sunshine, the springtime smells, the blue sky like the one on the day I took my first Communion.

The whole street was waking up. Life was beginning in houses more or less similar to ours. My wife went to open the street door to take in the bread and milk and I heard her talking to our next-door neighbor on the right, Madame Piedboeuf, the schoolmaster's wife. They had an ideal little girl, curly-haired and pink-cheeked, with big blue eyes and long doll's eyelashes, who was always dressed as if for a party, and for the past year they had had a little car in which they used to go for a drive every Sunday.

I don't know what the two women said to each other. From the noises I could hear, I gathered that they weren't the only ones outside, that women were calling to one another from doorstep to doorstep. When Jeanne came back, she looked pale and even more drawn than usual.

"They're going!" she told me.

"Where?"

"South, anywhere. At the end of the street I saw more cars going past with mattresses on the roof, Belgians mostly."

We had already seen them go by before Munich, and in October a certain number of Belgians had once again traveled to the south of France, rich people, who could wait.

"Do you intend to stay here?"

"I haven't the faintest idea."

I was telling the truth. I who had seen this event coming from so far away, who had waited for it for so long, I had not made any decisions in advance. It was as if I were waiting for a sign, as if I wanted Fate to decide for me.

I wasn't responsible anymore. Perhaps that's the word, perhaps that's what I was trying to explain just now. Only the day before, it had been up to me to manage my life and that of my family, to earn a living, to arrange for things to happen in the way things have to happen.

But not now. I had just lost my roots. I was no longer Marcel Féron, radio engineer in a newish district of Fumay, not far from the Meuse, but one man among millions whom superior forces were going to toss about at will.

I was no longer firmly attached to my house, to my habits. From one moment to the next, I had, so to speak, jumped into space.

From now on, decisions were no longer any concern of mine. Instead of my own palpitations, I was beginning to feel a sort of general palpitation. I wasn't living at my tempo anymore, but at the tempo of the radio, of the street, of the town which was waking up much faster than usual.

We ate in silence, in the kitchen, as usual, listening hard to the noises outside, without appearing to do so, on account of Sophie. Anyone would have thought that our daughter herself was hesitating to ask us any questions and she watched us in silence, one after the other.

"Drink your milk."

"Will we have any milk there?"

"What do you mean, there?"

"Why, where we are going…"

Tears started running down my wife's cheeks. She turned her head away while I looked sadly at the familiar walls, at the furniture which we had chosen piece by piece five years earlier, before we got married.

"Go and play now, Sophie."

And my wife, once she was alone with me, said:

"Perhaps I'd better go and see my father."

"What for?"

"To find out what they are doing."

She still had her father and mother, and three sisters, all married, two of whom lived at Fumay, one of them the wife of a confectioner in the Rue du Château.

It was because of her father that I had set up in business

on my own, for he was ambitious for his daughters and would not have allowed any of them to marry a workman.

It was he, too, who had made me buy the house on a twenty-year mortgage. I still had fifteen years of installments to pay, but in his eyes I was a property owner and that reassured him for the future.

"You never know what might happen to you, Marcel. You're cured, but people have been known to have relapses."

He had started in life as a miner in Delmotte's slate-pits, and had become a foreman. He had his own house too, and his own garden.

"You can arrange to buy a house in such a way that, if the husband happens to die, the wife doesn't have to pay anything more."

Wasn't it funny thinking about that on that particular morning, when nobody in the world could be sure of the future anymore?

Jeanne dressed and put on her hat.

"You'll keep an eye on Sophie, won't you?"

She went off to see her father. The cars went by, more and more of them, all heading south, and two or three times I thought I heard some planes. They didn't drop any bombs. Perhaps they were French or English: it was impossible to tell, for they were flying very high and the sun was dazzling.

I opened the shop while Sophie was playing in the yard. It isn't a real shop, for the house was not built for use as business premises. My customers have to go along a corridor and an ordinary window has to serve as a shop window. The same is true of the dairy shop, a little farther on. It is often like that in the suburbs, at least in the north. It means that we are forced to leave the front door open and I have fitted the shop door with a bell.

A couple of bargees came in for their radios. They weren't ready but they insisted on taking them all the same. One of them was going downstream toward Rethel, while the other, a Fleming, wanted to get home at all costs.

I washed and shaved, watching my daughter through the window from which I could see all the gardens in the street full of flowers and grass, which was still a fresh green. People were talking to each other over the walls and I could hear a conversation between the Matrays, on the same floor as I was, for the windows were open.

"How do you expect to take all that with you?"

"We'll need it."

"We may need it, but I don't see how we're going to carry those suitcases to the station."

"We'll take a taxi."

"If we can find one! I wonder if there'll still be any trains."

I was suddenly afraid. I pictured the crowds pouring down every street toward the little station just as the cars were streaming toward the south. It struck me that we ought to be leaving, that it was no longer a matter of hours but of minutes, and I reproached myself for having allowed my wife to go and see her father.

What advice could he give her? What did he know that I didn't?

The fact of the matter was that she had never ceased to belong to her family. She had married me, lived with me, given me one child, was going to give me another. She bore my name but remained a Van Straeten for all that, and the slightest thing was enough to send her running to see her parents or her sisters.

"I must go and ask Berthe's advice..."

Berthe was the confectioner's wife, the youngest of the

sisters and the one who had made the best match, which was probably why Jeanne regarded her as an oracle.

If we were leaving, it was time to go, I was sure of that, just as I was suddenly sure, without asking myself why, that we had to leave Fumay. I hadn't got a car, and for deliveries I used a handcart.

Without waiting for my wife to return, I went up to the attic to get the suitcases and a black trunk in which we kept old clothes.

"Are we taking the train, Daddy?"

"I think so."

"You aren't certain."

I was getting nervous. I felt angry with Jeanne for going out and was afraid that at any moment something might happen: anything, perhaps not yet the arrival of the German tanks in the town, but something like an air raid which would cut us off from each other.

Every now and then I went into Sophie's bedroom, which so to speak had never been used, since my daughter refused to sleep there, to look out into the street.

Outside three houses, including the house next door, cars were being loaded. The schoolmaster's daughter, Michèle, as curly-haired and fresh in her white dress as when she went to mass on Sunday, was holding a canary's cage while she waited for her parents to finish tying a mattress onto the roof of the car.

That reminded me of our hens and of Nestor, the cock Sophie was so fond of. It was I, three years earlier, who had put up some wire netting at the bottom of the garden and made a sort of henhouse.

Jeanne wanted fresh eggs for the child. Because of her father, of course, who had always kept hens, rabbits, and pigeons. He also had some carrier pigeons, and when there was a competition on a Sunday, he would spend motionless hours at the bottom of his garden waiting for his birds to return to the pigeon-house.

Our cock, two or three times a week, flew over the walls and I had to go from house to house looking for him. Some people complained of the damage he caused in their gardens, others of being waked up by his crowing.

"Can I take my dolly with me?"

"Yes."

"And the pram?"

"Not the pram. There won't be enough room in the train."

"Where's my dolly going to sleep?"

I very nearly snapped back that, only the night before, the doll had spent the night out in the yard. At last my wife came back.

"What you are doing?"

"I've started packing."

"You've decided to leave?"

"I think it's the best thing to do. What are your parents doing?"

"They're staying. My father has sworn not to leave his house, whatever happens. I dropped in at Berthe's too. They'll be on their way in a few minutes. They'll have to hurry, because it seems there are jams everywhere, especially Mézières' way. In Belgium, the Stukas are skimming the ground to machine-gun trains and cars."

She didn't protest at my decision because of her father, but didn't seem in any hurry to go. Perhaps she too would have preferred to cling to her house?

"They say there are peasants going off in their carts with

everything they can take with them, and driving their animals in front of them. I saw the station from a distance. It was swarming with people."

"What are you taking with you?"

"I don't know. Sophie's things, anyway. And we ought to take something to eat, especially for her. If you could find some condensed milk..."

I went to the grocer's in the next street, and, contrary to my expectations, there was nobody in the shop. It is true that most of the local people had stocked up back in October. The grocer, in his white apron, was as calm as usual and I felt slightly ashamed of my feverishness.

"Have you any condensed milk left?"

He pointed to a whole shelf full of tins.

"How much do you want?"

"A dozen tins?"

I expected him to refuse to sell me as many as that. I also bought several bars of chocolate, some ham, and a whole sausage. There were no standards left, no landmarks. Nobody was capable of saying what was going to be valuable or not.

At eleven o'clock we were still not ready and Jeanne delayed us still further by being sick. I hesitated. I felt sorry for her. I asked myself whether, in view of her condition, I had any right to take her off into the unknown. She didn't complain, bustling about and bumping her huge belly against the furniture and the door jambs.

"The hens!" she exclaimed all of a sudden.

Perhaps she had a vague hope that we would stay on account of the hens, but I had thought about them before her.

"Monsieur Reversé will take them in with his."

"They're staying, are they?"

"I'll dash around and ask him."

The Reversés lived on the quayside. They had two sons at the front and a daughter who was a nun in a convent at Givet.

"We are in God's hands," the old man told me. "If He is going to protect us, He will do it just as well here as anywhere else."

His wife, in the shadows, was telling her beads. I announced my intention of giving them my hens and my cock.

"How can I go and collect them?"

"I'll leave the key with you."

"It's a big responsibility."

I nearly decided to bring the birds around right away, but then I thought of the trains, of the crowd besieging the station, of the planes in the sky. This was no time to go running after poultry.

I had to insist.

"Even so, we shall probably never see anything we leave behind again..."

The idea didn't upset me. On the contrary, it filled me with a sort of somber joy, like that of destroying something you have patiently built up with your own hands.

What counted was going, was leaving Fumay. It didn't matter if, somewhere else, other dangers were waiting for us. True, we were running away. But as far as I was concerned, it wasn't from the Germans, from the bullets and bombs, from death.

After thinking carefully about it, I swear that that was how I felt. I had the impression that for other people this departure wasn't very important. For me, as I have already said, it was the hour of my meeting with Fate, the hour of an appointment which I had had a long time, which I had always had, with Fate.

Jeanne was sniveling as we left the house. Walking between the shafts of the handcart, I didn't even turn around. As I had finally informed Monsieur Reversé, to persuade him to take charge of my hens, I had left the house unlocked so that my customers could come and collect their radios if they wanted to. Just ordinary honesty on my part. And if anybody was going to steal something, wouldn't he have broken the door down anyway?

All that was over and done with. I pushed my handcart along and Jeanne walked along the pavement with Sophie, who was clutching her doll to her chest.

I had a hard time threading my way through the traffic jams, and once I thought I had lost my wife and daughter, until I found them a little farther on.

An army ambulance drove past at full speed with its siren wailing, and a little farther on I caught sight of a Belgian car which was pitted with bullet holes.

Other people, like us, were walking toward the station, burdened with suitcases and bundles. An old woman asked me if she might put hers on my cart, and she started pushing it along with me.

"Do you think we'll still get a train? Somebody told me the line was up."

"Where?"

"Near Dinant. My stepson, who works on the railways, has seen a trainload of wounded go by."

There was a rather wild look in most people's eyes, but that was chiefly the result of impatience. Everybody wanted to be off. It was all a matter of arriving in time. Everybody was convinced that part of the huge crowd would be left behind and sacrificed.

Were those who were not leaving taking greater risks?

Behind the windowpanes, faces were watching the fugitives, and it seemed to me, looking at them, that they were stamped with a sort of icy calm.

I knew the freight service buildings where I often used to go to collect parcels. I went in that direction, beckoning to my wife and daughter to follow me, and that was how we managed to get a train.

There were two in the station. One was a troop train full of disheveled soldiers grinning at the crowd.

Nobody was getting into the other train yet. Or rather, not everybody. Gendarmes were holding back the crowd. I had left my handcart. Young women wearing arm bands were bustling about, looking after the old people and the children.

One of them noticed my wife's belly, and our daughter whom she was holding by the hand.

"This way."

"But my husband…"

"The men will find room later on in the freight cars."

There was no arguing. You went where you were told, willy-nilly. Jeanne turned around, not knowing what was happening to her, trying to catch sight of me among all the heads. I shouted:

"Mademoiselle! Mademoiselle!"

The girl with the arm band came back toward me.

"Give her this. It's the little girl's food."

Indeed it was all the food we had brought with us.

I saw them get into a first-class carriage, and from the footboard Sophie waved to me—or, at least, in my direction, for she could not recognize me among the hundreds of faces.

I was jostled about. I felt in my pocket to make sure that

my spare pair of glasses were still there; those glasses which were my constant anxiety.

"Don't push!" cried a little man with a mustache.

And a gendarme repeated:

"Don't push. The train won't be leaving for another hour anyway!"

2

THE LADIES WITH THE ARM BANDS WENT ON
filling the carriages with an endless succession of old people, pregnant women, young children, and cripples, and I
was not the only one to wonder whether, in the end, there
would be any room on the train for the men. I looked forward with a certain irony to seeing my wife and daughter go
off while I was obliged to stay behind.

It was the gendarmes who finally got tired of holding
back the crowd. They suddenly broke the cordon and everybody rushed toward the five or six freight cars at the rear
of the train.

At the last minute I had given Jeanne, together with the
food, the suitcase containing Sophie's things and some of
hers. I was left with the heavier of the two suitcases, and with
my other hand I was dragging along as best I could the black
trunk, which was bumping against my legs at every step. I
didn't feel the pain. I wasn't thinking of anything, either.

I hoisted myself up, pushed by the people behind me,
and, trying to stay as near as possible to the sliding door, I
managed to put my trunk against the side of the car and sit
down on it, panting for breath, with the suitcase on my lap.

To begin with, I could see only the lower half of my
companions, men and women, and it was only later that

I made out their faces. At first I thought that I didn't know any of them, and that surprised me, for Fumay is a little town, with a population of about five thousand. It is true that some farm workers had come in from the surrounding country. A crowded district, which I didn't know very well, had emptied.

Everybody settled down hurriedly, ready to defend his space, and a voice shouted from the back of the car:

"Full up! Don't let any more in, you!"

There was some nervous laughter, the first, and that reduced the tension slightly. The first contact had already become easier. Everybody started making himself comfortable, arranging his suitcases and bundles around him.

The sliding doors on both sides of the car had been left open, and we looked without much interest at the crowd waiting on the platform for another train, the refreshment room and the bar being pillaged, the bottles of beer and wine being passed from hand to hand.

"Hey, you over there... Yes, you, Ginger... You couldn't go and get me a bottle, could you?"

For a moment I thought of going to see how my wife and daughter had settled down, and at the same time reassure them with the news that I had found a place; I didn't do so for fear of not finding it on my return.

We didn't wait an hour, as the gendarme had said, but two and a half hours.

Several times the train gave a shudder and the buffers bumped against one another, and every time we held our breath, hoping that we were moving off at last. Once, it was because some cars were being added to the train.

The men who were close to the open doors reported on what was happening to those who could not see anything.

"They're adding at least eight cars. The train stretches at least halfway round the bend now."

A sort of fellowship was being established between those who had found a place on the train and were more or less sure of getting away.

One man, who had jumped down onto the platform, counted the carriages and freight cars.

"Twenty-eight!" he announced.

We didn't care a jot about the people stranded on the platforms and outside the station. The next rush was no concern of ours, and indeed we hoped that the train would go before it started.

We saw an old lady in a wheelchair being pushed along by a nurse toward the first-class carriages. She was wearing a mauve hat and a little white veil, and she had white thread gloves on her hands.

Later on, some stretchers were carried in the same direction, and I wondered whether people already in the carriages were going to be turned out, for a rumor started spreading that the hospital was being evacuated.

I was thirsty. Two of my neighbors dropped onto the line, ran over to the platform, and came back with bottles of beer. I didn't dare imitate them.

Little by little I started getting used to the faces around me, old men, for the most part, for the others had been called up, working-class women and country women, a fifteen-year-old boy with a long scraggy neck, and a girl of nine or ten whose hair was tied with a shoelace.

I finally recognized somebody after all, indeed two people. First Fernand Leroy, who had been at school with me and had become a clerk at Hachette's bookshop, next door to the confectioner's run by my sister-in-law.

From the other end of the car, where he was wedged in a corner, he gave me a little wave which I returned although I had had no occasion to speak to him for years.

As for the second person, he was a picturesque Fumay character, an old drunkard whom everybody called Jules and who distributed handbills outside the movie houses.

It took me some time to identify a third face, even though it was nearer to me, because it was hidden from me by a man with shoulders twice as broad. This third person was a buxom woman of about thirty, who was already eating a sandwich, a certain Julie who ran a little café near the port.

She was wearing a blue serge skirt, which was too tight and riding up her hips, and a white blouse marked with rings of sweat, through which you could see her brassiere.

She smelled of powder and perfume, and I remember seeing her lipstick coming off onto the bread.

The troop train moved off toward the north. A few minutes later we heard a train approaching on the same line, and somebody shouted:

"Now it's coming back!"

It wasn't the same one, but a Belgian train even more crowded than ours and with only civilians on it. There were even people standing on the footboards.

Some of them jumped onto our cars. The gendarmes came running up, shouting orders. The loudspeaker joined in, announcing that nobody was allowed to leave his place.

All the same, a few managed to get in on the wrong side of the train, among them a young brunette in a black dress covered with dust, who was carrying no luggage and hadn't even a handbag.

She climbed shyly into our car, pale-faced, sad-looking, and nobody said anything to her. One or two men just exchanged winks while she huddled in a corner.

We couldn't see the cars anymore and I am sure that none of us cared. Those who were near the doors looked at nothing but the piece of sky which was visible, a sky as blue as ever, wondering whether a German squadron might not appear at any moment and start bombing the station.

Since the arrival of the Belgian train, it was rumored that some stations had been bombed on the other side of the frontier, according to certain people the station at Namur.

I wish I could convey the atmosphere and above all the state of suspense in our car. We were beginning, in the stationary train, to form a little world on its own, but which remained, so to speak, in a state of tension.

Cut off from the rest, it was as if our group was only waiting for a signal, a whistle, a hiss of steam, the sound of the wheels on the rails, to fall back entirely upon itself.

And that finally happened, when we were beginning to give up hope.

What would my companions have done if they had been told that the line was blocked, that the trains had stopped running? Would they have gone home with their bundles?

Speaking for myself, I don't think that I would have given up: I think I would rather have walked along the track. It was too late to turn back. The break had occurred. The idea of going back to my street, my house, my workshop, my garden, my habits, the labeled radios waiting on the shelves to be repaired, struck me as unbearable.

The crowd on the platform started slipping slowly behind us, and for me it was as if it had never existed, as if the town itself, where, except for the four years in the sanatorium, I had spent my life, had lost its reality.

I didn't give a thought to Jeanne and my daughter sitting

in their first-class carriage, farther from me than if they had been hundreds of miles away.

I didn't wonder what they were doing, how they had borne the long wait, or whether Jeanne had been sick again.

I was more concerned about my spare pair of glasses, and every time one of my companions moved I protected my pocket with my hand.

Just outside the town we passed, on the left, the state forest of Manise, where we had spent so many Sunday afternoons on the grass. To my eyes, it was not the same forest, possibly because I was seeing it from the railway. The broom was growing thickly and the train was moving so slowly that I could see the bees buzzing from flower to flower.

All of a sudden the train stopped and we all looked at one another with the same fear in our eyes. A railwayman ran along the track. Finally he shouted something I didn't understand and the train moved off again.

I wasn't hungry. I had forgotten my thirst. I looked at the grass passing by a few yards away, sometimes only a foot or two, and the wild flowers, white, blue, and yellow, whose names I didn't know and which I felt I was seeing for the first time. Whiffs of Julie's perfume reached me, especially on the bends, mingled with the strong but not unpleasant smell of her sweat.

Her café was like my shop. It wasn't a real café. There were curtains in the windows which, when they were drawn, made it impossible to make out anything inside.

The bar was tiny, without either a metal top or a sink behind. The shelf, with five or six bottles on it, was just a kitchen fitting.

I had often glanced inside when I was passing, and I remember, on the wall, next to a cuckoo clock which didn't work and the notice about the law on drunkenness in public, a publicity calendar showing a blonde holding a glass of foaming beer. A glass shaped like a champagne glass, that was what struck me.

That isn't interesting, I know. I mention it because I thought of it at that moment. There were other smells in our car, not counting that of the car itself, which had carried some cattle on one of its recent trips and smelled of the farmyard.

Some of my companions were eating sausages or pâté. One country girl had brought a huge cheese with her and kept cutting into it with a kitchen knife.

So far we had exchanged only inquisitive glances, which were still cautious, and only those who came from the same village or the same district were talking, generally to identify the places we were passing.

"Look! Dédé's farm! I wonder if he's staying. His cows are in the meadow, anyway."

We went through stops and deserted little stations where there were baskets of flowers hanging from the lamps and travel posters on the walls.

"Look, Corsica! Why don't we go to Corsica?"

After Revin we went faster, and before arriving at Monthermé we saw a lime kiln and more rows of working-class houses.

Just as we were entering the station, the engine gave a piercing whistle like a big express. Passing the station buildings and the platforms swarming with troops, it drew up in a setting of deserted tracks and signal boxes.

A pump, next to our car, was oozing huge drops of water, one by one, and I felt my thirst coming on again. A peasant, jumping down from the train, urinated on the next track, out in the sunshine, with one eye on the engine. This made everybody laugh. We felt a need to laugh, and some of the men started cracking jokes on purpose. Old Jules was asleep, with a half-empty bottle in one hand and his haversack, containing more bottles, on his belly.

"They're uncoupling the engine!" announced the man who was relieving himself.

Two or three others got out. I still didn't dare. It seemed to me that I had to hang on at all costs, that it was particularly important for me.

A quarter of an hour later, another engine was pulling us in the opposite direction, but, instead of going through Monthermé, we took a side track running alongside the Semois toward Belgium.

I had made this trip before, with Jeanne, before she became my wife. I even wonder whether it wasn't that day, a Sunday in August, which decided our fate.

Marriage at that time didn't mean the same to me as to somebody normal. Has there been anything really normal in my life since that evening when I saw my mother come home naked and with her hair cropped?

Yet it wasn't even that event which struck me. At the time I didn't understand or try to understand. For the past four years so many things had been put down to the war that one more mystery was not likely to upset me.

Madame Jamais, our landlady, was a widow and earned a good living as a dressmaker. She looked after me for about a fortnight, until my father came home. I didn't recognize him at first. He was still wearing uniform, a different uniform from the one in which he had gone away; his mustache smelled of sour wine; his eyes were shining as if he had a cold in the head.

The fact was, I scarcely knew him, and the only photograph we had of him, on the sideboard, was the one taken with my mother on their wedding day. I still wonder why both their faces were lopsided. Perhaps Sophie finds that in our wedding photograph our features too are lopsided?

I knew that he had worked as a clerk for Monsieur Sauveur, the dealer in seeds and fertilizers whose offices and warehouses, occupying a long stretch of the quayside, were linked by a private track to the freight station.

My mother had pointed Monsieur Sauveur out to me in the street, a rather short, fat man with a very pale face, who must have been sixty at the time and walked slowly, cautiously, as if he were afraid of the slightest shock.

"He's got a heart disease. He may drop dead in the street any minute. The last time he had an attack, they only just managed to save him, and afterward they had to call in a great specialist from Paris."

When I was a little boy I sometimes followed him with my eyes, wondering whether the accident was going to happen in front of me. I couldn't understand how, with a threat like that hanging over him, Monsieur Sauveur could come and go like everybody else without looking sad.

"Your father is his right-hand man. He started working for him as an office boy, at the age of sixteen, and now he can sign for the firm."

Sign what? I found out later that my father was in fact the managing clerk and that his position was just as important as my mother had said.

He went back to his old job, and we gradually got used to living together in our flat, where my mother was never mentioned, although the wedding photograph remained on the sideboard.

It had taken me some time to understand why my father's mood changed so much from one day to the next, sometimes from one hour to the next. He could be very affectionate and sentimental, taking me on his knees, which rather embarrassed me, and telling me with tears in his eyes that I was all he had in life, that that was enough for him, that nothing mattered in life but a son....

Then, a few hours later, he would seem surprised to find me at home and would order me about as if I were a maid, bullying me and shouting at me that I was no better than my mother.

Finally I heard that he drank, or to be more precise that he had started drinking, out of grief, when he hadn't found his wife waiting for him on his return and when he had heard what had happened.

I believed that for a long time. Then I thought about it. I remembered the day of his arrival, his shining eyes, his jerky gestures, his smell, the bottles which he went to the grocer's to get right away.

I caught odd phrases when he was talking about the war with his friends, and I guessed that it was at the front that he had got into the habit of drinking.

I don't hold it against him. I have never held it against him, even when, reeling about and muttering swear-words, he would bring home a woman he had picked up in the street and lock me in my room.

I didn't like Madame Jamais wheedling me and treating me like a victim. I avoided her. I had got into the habit of going shopping after school, cooking the meals, doing the washing-up.

One evening, a couple of passersby brought in my father, whom they had found lying unconscious on the pavement.

I wanted to go for a doctor but they said that that wasn't necessary, that all my father needed was to sleep it off. I helped them to undress him.

Monsieur Sauveur only kept him on out of pity, I knew that too. Several times he was insulted by his managing clerk, who, the next day, would beg his forgiveness with tears in his eyes.

That isn't really important. What I wanted to show was that I didn't lead the same kind of life as other children of my age and that when I was fourteen I had to be sent to a sanatorium above Saint-Gervais in Savoy.

When I set off, alone on my train—it was the first time I had ever taken a train—I was convinced that I wasn't going to come back alive. This idea didn't make me sad, and I began to understand Monsieur Sauveur's serenity.

In any case, I would never be like other men. Already, at school, my poor sight had prevented me from playing any games. And now, on top of that, I was suffering from a disease which was regarded as a taint, a disease which was almost shameful. What woman would ever agree to marry me?

I spent four years up there, rather like here in the train; I mean that the past and future didn't count, nor what was happening in the valley, still less in the faraway towns.

When I was declared to be cured and sent back to Fumay, I was eighteen. I found my father more or less as I had left him, except that his features were softer, his eyes sad and frightened.

When he saw me, he studied my reaction and I realized that he was ashamed, that in his heart of hearts he wished I hadn't come back.

I had to find a sedentary occupation. I started work as

an apprentice to Monsieur Ponchot, who ran the town's big piano, record, and radio shop.

In the mountains, I had got into the habit of reading up to two books a day, and I kept it up. Every month, then every three months, I went to a specialist at Mézières to be examined, never trusting his reassuring words.

I had returned to Fumay in 1926. My father died in 1934, from a clot of blood, while Monsieur Sauveur was still going strong. I had just met Jeanne, who was an assistant in Choblet's glove shop, two doors away from where I worked.

I was twenty-six; she was twenty-two. We walked along the streets in the twilight. We went together to the movies, where I held her hand, then, on Sunday afternoon, I obtained permission to take her into the country.

That struck me as incredible. For me, she was not just a woman, but the symbol of a normal regular life.

And it was, I would swear to it, in the course of that outing in the Semois valley, for which I had had to ask her father's permission, that I acquired the assurance that it was possible, that she was ready to marry me, to start a family with me.

I was speechless with gratitude. I would gladly have gone on my knees at her feet. If I talk about it at such length, it is in order to emphasize Jeanne's importance in my eyes.

Now, in my cattle car, I didn't give a thought to her, a woman seven and a half months pregnant, for whom this journey must have been particularly difficult. My thoughts were elsewhere. I wondered why we were being shunted down a side track which led nowhere, except to a place more dangerous than the one we had just left.

As we were stopping in the open country, near a grade

crossing which cut across a minor road, I heard someone say:

"They're clearing the lines to let the troop trains through. They must need reinforcements out there."

The train didn't move. We couldn't hear anything except, all of a sudden, birds singing and the murmur of a spring. One man jumped onto the bank, followed by another.

"Hey there, guard, are we going to stay here long?"

"An hour or two. Unless we spend the night here."

"The train isn't likely to move off without warning, is it?"

"The engine is going back to Monthermé, and they're sending us another from there."

I made sure that the engine really was being uncoupled; then, when I saw it go off by itself in a landscape of woods and meadows, I jumped down onto the ground, and, before doing anything else, went to have a drink at the spring, in the hollow of my hand, as I used to when I was little. The water had the same taste as it had then, the taste of grass and my own hot body.

People were getting out of all the carriages. Hesitant at first, then more self-assured, I started walking alongside the train, trying to see inside.

"Daddy!"

My daughter was calling me and waving.

"Where's your mother?"

"Here."

Two elderly women were blocking the view and would not have moved for all the gold in the world, scowling disapprovingly at my daughter's excitement.

"Open the door, Daddy. I can't manage. Mummy wants to talk to you."

The carriage was an old model. I succeeded in opening

the door and was confronted with eight people in two rows, as grim and motionless as in a dentist's waiting room. My wife and daughter were the only ones under sixty, and an old man in the far corner was clearly a nonagenarian.

"Are you all right, Marcel?"

"Yes. What about you?"

"I'm all right. I was wondering what you were going to eat. Luckily, we've stopped. You see, we've got all the food."

Wedged between two women with monumental hips, she could scarcely move, and she had some difficulty in handing me a thin loaf of bread together with the whole sausage.

"But what about you two?"

"You know perfectly well we can't stand garlic."

"Is there some garlic in it?"

That morning, at the grocer's, I hadn't bothered to make sure.

"How are you fixed?"

"All right."

"You couldn't get me some water, could you? They gave me a bottle before we left, but it's so hot here that we've already drunk it all."

She handed me a bottle and I ran to the spring to fill it. There, on her knees, washing her face, I found the young woman in the black dress who had got in on the wrong side of the car after the arrival of the Belgian train.

"Where did you find a bottle?" she asked me.

Her accent was neither Belgian nor German.

"Somebody gave it to my wife."

She didn't press the point, but wiped her face with her handkerchief, and I went off toward the first-class carriage.

On the way I stumbled over an empty beer bottle and

turned back to pick it up as if it were a precious object. My wife jumped to the wrong conclusion.

"Are you drinking beer?"

"No. It's to put some water in."

It was curious. We were talking to each other like strangers. Not exactly: rather, like distant relatives who haven't seen each other for a long time and don't know what to say. Perhaps it was because of the presence of the old women.

"Can I get out, Daddy?"

"If you like."

My wife looked worried.

"What if the train starts moving?"

"We haven't got an engine anymore."

"You mean we're going to stay here?"

At that moment we heard the first explosion, a muffled, distant sound, but one which nonetheless made us jump, and one of the old women made the sign of the cross and shut her eyes as if she had heard a clap of thunder.

"What's that?"

"I don't know."

"You can't see any planes?"

I looked at the sky, which was as blue as it had been that morning, with just two gilded clouds floating slowly along.

"Don't let her go far, Marcel."

"I won't let her out of my sight."

Holding Sophie by the hand, I walked along the tracks looking for another bottle, and I was lucky enough to find one, bigger than the first.

"What are you going to do with it?"

I told a half lie.

"I'm collecting them."

For I was just picking up a third bottle which had

contained some wine. My intention was to give at least one to the young woman in black.

I could see her from a distance, standing in front of our car, and her dusty satin dress, her figure, her tousled hair seemed foreign to everything around her. She was stretching her legs without paying any attention to what was happening and I noticed her high, pointed heels.

"Your mother hasn't been sick?"

"No. There's a woman who talks all the time and she says the train is sure to be bombed. Is that true?"

"She doesn't know anything about it."

"You don't think it'll be bombed?"

"I'm sure it won't."

"Where are we going to sleep?"

"In the train."

"There aren't any beds."

I went and washed the three bottles, rinsing them several times to remove as far as possible the taste of the beer and the wine, and filled them with fresh water.

I went back to my car, still accompanied by Sophie, and handed one of the bottles to the young woman.

She looked at me in surprise, looked at my daughter, thanked me with a nod of her head, and climbed up into the car to put it in a safe place.

There was only one house in sight, apart from the one belonging to the grade-crossing keeper: a tiny farm, a fair way away, on the hillside, and in the yard a woman with a blue apron was feeding the hens as if the war didn't exist.

"Is that where you are? On the floor?"

"I sit on the trunk."

Julie was at grips with a red-faced man with thick, gray hair who was giving her meaningful looks, and every now and then the two of them burst into the sort of laughter you hear in the arbors of tavern gardens. The man had a bottle of red wine in his hand and kept giving his companion a swig from it. There were purple stains on her blouse, inside of which her big breasts bounced about with every burst of laughter.

"Let's go back to your mother."

"Already?"

New subdivisions were beginning to take shape. On one side there was the world of the passenger carriages and on the other there was ours, the world of the cattle cars and the freight cars. Jeanne and my daughter belonged to the first world, I to the second, and I unconsciously showed some haste in taking Sophie back.

"Aren't you going to eat?"

I ate my bread and sausage, on the track, in front of the open door. We could not say very much to one another, with those two rows of frozen faces whose eyes kept moving from my wife to me and my daughter.

"Do you think we'll set off again soon?"

"They have to let the troop trains through. Once the line is clear, it will be our turn. Look! The engine's arriving."

We could hear it, then see it, all by itself, with its white smoke, following the bends of the valley.

"Hurry back to your place. I'm so frightened that somebody might have taken it!"

Relieved to get away, I kissed Sophie but didn't dare to kiss Jeanne in front of everybody. A spiteful voice called after me:

"You might at least shut the door!"

Nearly every Sunday in summer, first with Jeanne, then with her and my daughter, I used to go into the country to have a snack and sometimes lunch on the grass.

But it wasn't the smell or the taste of that countryside which I was rediscovering today but the smell and the taste of my childhood memories.

For years I had sat down every Sunday in a clearing, I had played there with Sophie, I had picked flowers to make garlands for her, but all that was, so to speak, neutral.

Why was it that today the world had recovered its savor?

Even the buzzing of the wasps reminded me of the buzzing I heard when I used to hold my breath and watch a bee circling around my bread and butter.

The faces, when I got back into the car, seemed more familiar. A sort of complicity was growing up between us, making us wink, for instance, after watching the antics of Julie and her horse dealer.

I say horse dealer without knowing. People's names didn't matter, nor their occupation. He looked like a horse dealer and that was what I called him to myself.

The couple were holding each other around the waist, and the man's big hand was squeezing Julie's breast when the train started moving again after a few jolts.

The woman in black, who was still pressed against the side of the car, a few feet away from me, had nothing to sit on. It is true that, like so many others, she could have sat down on the floor. There were even four people in one corner who were playing cards as if they were sitting around a table in an inn.

We returned to Monthermé, and a little later I caught a glimpse of Leversy Lock, where a dozen motor barges were vibrating on the dazzling water. The bargees had no need of a train, but the locks were there to stop them and I could imagine their impatience.

The sky was turning pink. Three planes went over, flying very low, with reassuring tricolor roundels. They were so close that we could make out the face of one of the pilots. I could have sworn that he waved to us.

When we arrived at Mézières, dusk had fallen, and our train, instead of going into the station, drew up in a wilderness of tracks. A soldier whose rank I didn't see went along the train shouting:

"Nobody must get out! It is absolutely forbidden to leave the train."

There was no platform anyway, and a little later some guns mounted on open trucks went past us at full speed. They had scarcely disappeared before the siren sounded an air-raid warning while the same voice went on shouting:

"Stay where you are. It's dangerous to get off the train. Stay where you are..."

Now we could hear the drone of a certain number of planes. The town was in darkness and in the station, where all the lights were out, the passengers were probably running into the subways.

I don't think that I was frightened. I sat perfectly still, staring at the faces opposite me, and listening to the sound of the engines, which grew louder and then seemed to fade away.

There was complete silence and our train stayed there, as if abandoned in the middle of a complicated network of tracks on which a few empty carriages were standing about. Among others, I can remember a tanker which bore in big yellow letters the name of a Montpellier wine merchant.

Despite ourselves, we remained in suspense, not saying anything, waiting for the all-clear, which was not sounded for almost another half hour. During this time, the horse dealer's hand had left Julie's breast. It settled there again, more insistent than before, and the man pressed his lips on his neighbor's.

A countrywoman muttered:

"Disgusting, I call it, in front of a little girl."

And he retorted, his mouth daubed with lipstick:

"The little girl will have to learn one day! Didn't you ever learn, in your day?"

This was the sort of coarse, vulgar remark to which I wasn't accustomed. It reminded me of the torrent of abuse my mother had poured on the youths who had followed her, jeering at her. I glanced at the dark-haired girl. She was looking somewhere else as if she hadn't heard, and didn't notice my interest.

I have never been drunk for the simple reason that I drink neither wine nor beer. But I imagine that when night fell I was in roughly the condition of a man who has had a drop too much.

Possibly on account of the afternoon sun, in the valley with the spring, my eyelids were hot and prickly; I felt that my cheeks were red, my arms and legs numb, my mind empty.

I gave a start when somebody, striking a match to look at his watch, announced in an undertone:

"Half past ten…!"

Time was passing at once fast and slowly. To tell the truth, there was no time anymore.

Some of my companions were asleep, others were talking in low voices. I dozed off, for my part, on the black trunk, with my head against the side of the car, and later on, in a half sleep, while the train was still motionless, surrounded by darkness and silence, I became aware of rhythmical movements close beside me. It took me some time to realize that it was Julie and her companion making love.

I wasn't shocked, even though, possibly on account of my disease, I have always been rather prudish. I followed the rhythm as if it were music and I must admit that, little by little, a detailed picture took shape in my mind, and the whole of my body was filled with a diffused warmth.

When I dropped off to sleep again, Julie was murmuring, probably to another neighbor of hers:

"No! Not now!"

A long time afterward, toward the middle of the night, a series of jolts shook us, as if our train were shunting about. People were walking up and down the line, talking. Somebody said:

"It's the only way."

And somebody else:

"I'll only take orders from the military commandant."

They went off arguing and the train started moving, only to halt again after a few minutes.

I stopped taking any notice of these movements which I couldn't understand. We had left Fumay, and, provided we didn't go back, the rest was a matter of indifference to me.

There were some whistle blasts, more jolts, more halts followed by the hissing of steam.

I know nothing about what happened that night at Mézières or anywhere else in the world, except that there was fighting in Holland and Belgium, that tens of thousands of people were crowding the roads, that planes were streaking across the sky nearly everywhere, and that the anti-aircraft guns fired a few random shots every now and then. We heard some bursts of gunfire, in the distance, and an endless convoy of trucks, on a road which must have passed close to the railway.

In our car, where it was pitch-dark, the sound of snoring created a curious intimacy. Now and then somebody in an uncomfortable position or having a nightmare would give an unwitting groan.

When I finally opened my eyes, we were moving, and half my companions were awake. A milky dawn was breaking, lighting up a countryside which was unfamiliar to me, fairly high hills covered with woods and farmhouses standing in huge clearings.

Julie was asleep, her mouth half open, her blouse undone. The young woman in the black dress was sitting with her back against the side of the car, and a lock of hair hanging over one cheek. I wondered whether she had stayed like that all night and whether she had been able to sleep. Her eyes met mine. She smiled at me, on account of the bottle of water.

"Where are we?" asked one of my neighbors, waking up.

"I don't know," answered the man sitting in the doorway with his legs hanging out. "We've just passed a station called Lafrancheville. "

We passed another decked with flowers and deserted like the rest. On the blue-and-white sign I read the name: BOULZICOURT.

The train started rounding a bend, through some fairly flat country; the man with the dangling legs took his pipe out of his mouth to exclaim in comical despair:

"Hell!"

"What is it?"

"The swine have shortened the train!"

"What's that you say?"

There was a rush toward the door, and, hanging on with both hands, the man protested:

"Stop pushing, you! You're going to shove me out on the line. You can see for yourselves there are only five carriages in front of us. Well, what have they done with the others? And how am I going to find my wife and kids? Hell! Oh, damn it to hell!"

3

"I KNEW PERFECTLY WELL THAT THE ENGINE couldn't pull all those carriages. They must have realized that in the end and decided to cut the train in two."

"The first thing to do was to tell us, wasn't it? What's going to happen to the women?"

"Perhaps they're waiting for us at Rethel. Or at Rheims."

"Unless they're going to give them back to us, like soldiers' wives, when this damned war finishes—if it ever does!"

I tried automatically to distinguish between sincerity and sham in these angry complaints. Wasn't this above all a sort of game these men were playing with themselves, because there were witnesses?

Personally I wasn't upset, nor really anxious. I stayed where I was, motionless, a little startled in spite of everything. Suddenly I had the feeling that a pair of eyes were gazing insistently at me.

I was right. The face of the woman in black was turned toward me, paler in the dawn light, and not as clear-cut as the day before. She was trying, with her gaze, to convey a message of sympathy to me, and at the same time I had the impression that she was asking a question.

I interpreted it as:

"How are you standing up to the shock? Are you terribly upset?"

This put me in a quandary. I didn't dare to show her my lack of concern, which she would have misinterpreted. I accordingly assumed a sad expression, but without overdoing it. She had seen me on the track with my daughter and must have deduced that my wife was with me too. As far as she could see, I had just lost them both, temporarily, but lost them nonetheless.

"Courage!" her brown eyes said to me over the others' heads.

I responded with the smile of a sick man whom somebody is trying to reassure but who feels no better as a result. I am almost certain that if we had been closer to one another she would have given my hand a furtive squeeze.

In behaving like that, I didn't intend to deceive her, as one might imagine, but, with all those heads between us, it wasn't the time to explain how I felt.

Later on, if we happened to be brought together and if she gave me the opportunity, I would tell her the truth, since I wasn't ashamed of it.

I was no more surprised by what was happening to us than I had been, the day before, on hearing of the invasion of Holland and the Ardennes. On the contrary, my idea that it was a matter between Fate and myself was reinforced. It was becoming more obvious. I had been separated from my family, which was a personal attack and no mistake.

The sky was rapidly brightening, as pure and clear as the day before when, in my garden, I had been feeding the hens without knowing that it was the last time.

I was touched by the memory of my hens, and the

mental picture of Nestor, his comb all crimson, struggling fiercely when old Monsieur Reversé tried to grab him.

I imagined the scene between the two low, whitewashed walls, the beating of the wings, the white feathers flying, the vicious pecks, and perhaps Monsieur Matray, if he had been prevented from leaving, climbing onto his crate to look over the wall and give advice as he usually did.

That didn't prevent me from thinking at the same time about this woman who had just shown sympathy for me when I had done nothing but give her an empty bottle picked up from the track.

While she was doing her hair with her fingers moistened with saliva, I tried to decide to what category she belonged. I couldn't make up my mind. I told myself that it didn't really matter and eventually the idea occurred to me of handing her the comb I had in my pocket, while my neighbor whom I was disturbing gave me a meaningful look.

He was mistaken. I wasn't doing it for that.

We were moving fairly slowly and out in the open country when we began to hear a steady buzz which we didn't manage to place immediately, and which was just a vibration of the air to begin with.

"There they are!" exclaimed the man with the pipe, his legs still dangling in the air.

For somebody who never felt giddy, he had the best place in the car.

I discovered later on that he was a constructional ironworker.

Bending down, I saw them too, for I wasn't far from the door. The man was counting:

"Nine... ten... eleven... twelve... there are twelve of them... probably what they call a squadron. If it was the

right time of the year and they weren't making any noise, I'd
swear they were storks…."

I counted eleven of them, high up in the sky. Because of
a trick of the light, they appeared white and luminous, and
they were flying in a V-shaped formation.

"What's that fellow up to?"

Pressed against one another, we were looking up at the
sky when I felt the woman's hand on my shoulder where she
might easily have put it inadvertently.

The last plane in one leg of the V had just broken away
from the others and seemed to be diving toward the ground,
so that our first impression was that it was falling. It grew
larger at incredible speed, spiraling down, while the others, instead of continuing on their way toward the horizon,
started forming a huge circle.

The rest happened so quickly that we didn't have time
to be really frightened. The plane which was doing the nose
dive had disappeared from our sight, but we could hear its
menacing roar.

It flew over the train, along its whole length, from back
to front, so low that we instinctively ducked.

Then it disappeared only to repeat its maneuver, with
the difference that this time we heard the rattle of the machine gun above us, and other sounds, like that of wood
splintering.

There were shouts, inside our car and elsewhere. The
train went a little farther, then, like a wounded animal,
stopped after a few jolts.

For a while there was complete silence, the silence of
fear, which I was facing for the first time, and I was probably
not breathing any more than my companions.

All the same, I went on looking at the scene in the sky,

the plane soaring upwards again, its two swastikas clearly
visible, the head of the pilot giving us a final glance, and the
others, up there, circling around until he took up his position again.

"Swine!"

I don't know from whose breast the word exploded. It
relieved us all and roused us from our immobility.

A little girl was crying. A woman pushed forward, repeating as if she didn't know what she was saying:

"Let me pass… Let me pass."

"Are you hurt?"

"My husband…"

"Where is he?"

Everybody looked instinctively for a body stretched out
on the floor.

"In the next car.… The one that's been hit… I heard
it.…"

Her face drawn, she dropped to the stones beside the
lines and started running along, shouting:

"François!… François!"

None of us made a pretty picture and we felt no desire
to look at one another. It seemed to me that everything was
happening in slow motion, but perhaps that was just an
illusion. I also remember something like zones of silence
around isolated noises which sounded even louder as a
result.

One man, then another, then a third jumped down,
and their first instinct was to pass water without taking the
trouble to move away, or even, in one case, to face the other
way.

Farther off a continuous lament could be heard, a sort
of animal howl.

As for Julie, she stood up, her blouse coming out of her crumpled skirt, and said in a drunken voice:

"Well, chum!"

She repeated this two or three times; perhaps she was still repeating it when I got out in my turn and helped the woman in black to jump down onto the ground.

Why was it that particular moment that I asked her:

"What's your name?"

She didn't consider the question stupid or out of place, for she answered:

"Anna."

She didn't ask me what I was called. I told her all the same:

"My name is Marcel. Marcel Féron."

I would have liked to pass water like the others. I didn't dare, because of her, and it hurt me to restrain myself.

There was a meadow below the track, with tall grass, barbed wire, and, a hundred yards away, a white farmhouse where there was nobody to be seen. Some hens, around a pile of manure, had all started cackling together, as excited as if they had been frightened too.

The people in the other car had got out, as flustered and awkward as we were.

In front of one of the carriages there was a more compact, solemn crowd. Some faces were turned away.

"A woman has been wounded over there," somebody came and told us. "I don't suppose there's a doctor among you?"

Why did the question strike me as grotesque? Do doctors travel in cattle cars? Could any of us be taken for a doctor?

At the front of the train, the fireman, his face and hands

black, was waving his arms about, and a little later we learned that the engineer had been killed by a bullet in the face.

"They're coming back! They're coming back!"

The shout ended in a strangled cry. Everybody copied the first ones who had had the idea of throwing themselves flat on their faces in the meadow, at the foot of the embankment.

I did like the others; so did Anna, who was now following me about like a dog without a master.

The planes up in the sky were forming another circle, a little farther west, and this time we missed nothing of the maneuver. We saw one plane come spiraling down, flatten out just when it seemed bound to crash, skim the ground, soar upward again, and sweep around to cover the same ground once more, this time firing its machine gun.

It was two or three miles away. We couldn't see the target—a village, perhaps, or a road—which was hidden by a wood of fir trees. And already it was climbing into the sky to join the flock waiting for it up there and follow them northward.

I went, like the others, to look at the dead engineer, part of his body on the footplate, near the open firebox, his head and shoulders hanging over the side. There was no face left, just a black and red mass from which the blood was oozing in big drops onto the gray stones by the track.

He was my first dead man of the war. He was almost my first dead man, apart from my father, who had been laid out by the time I came home.

I felt sick and tried not to show it, because Anna was beside me, and because at that moment she took my arm

as naturally as a girl walking along the street with her
sweetheart.

I think she was less upset than I was. And yet I myself
was less upset than I would have expected. At the sanatorium, where there were a lot of dead people, we were not
allowed to see them. The nurses acted in good time, coming
to collect a patient from his bed, sometimes in the middle of
the night. We knew what that meant.

There was a special room for dying, and another, in
the basement, where the body was kept until the relatives
claimed it or it was buried in the little local cemetery.

Those deaths were different. There wasn't the sunshine,
the grass, the flowers, the cackling hens, the flies buzzing
around our heads.

"We can't leave him there."

The men looked at one another. Two of them, both elderly, volunteered to lend the fireman a hand.

I don't know where they put the engineer. Walking back
along the train, I noticed holes in the sides of the cars, long
scores which showed the wood as bare as when you fell a
tree.

A woman had been wounded, one shoulder, we were
told, practically torn off.

It was she whom we could hear groaning as if she were
in labor. There were just a few other women around her, old
women for the most part, for the men, embarrassed, had
moved away in silence.

"It isn't a pretty sight."

"What are we going to do? Stay here until they come
back to snipe at us?"

I saw an old man sitting on the ground, holding a blood-
stained handkerchief to his face. A bottle, hit by a bullet,

had shattered in his hand and splinters of glass had scored his cheeks. He didn't complain. I could see only his eyes, which were expressing nothing but a sort of amazement.

"They've found somebody to attend to her."

"Who?"

"A midwife on the train."

I caught sight of her, a sour-faced little old woman with a sturdy figure and her hair arranged in a bun on top of her head. She didn't belong to our car.

Without realizing, we gathered together in groups corresponding to the carriages, and in front of ours the man with the pipe went on protesting halfheartedly. He was one of the few who had not been to see the dead engineer.

"What the hell are we waiting for? Isn't there a single bastard here who can make that damned engine work?"

I remember somebody climbing up onto the track carrying a dead chicken by the feet, and sitting down to pluck it. I didn't try to understand. Seeing that nothing was happening as it did in ordinary life, everything was natural.

"The fireman wants a hefty fellow to feed the boiler while he tries to take the engineer's place. He thinks he can manage. It isn't as if the traffic was normal."

Contrary to all expectations, the horse dealer volunteered, without making a song and dance about it. It seemed to amuse him, like those members of an audience who go up onto the stage in response to an appeal by a conjuror.

He took off his jacket, his tie, and his wristwatch, which he handed over to Julie before making for the engine.

The half-plucked chicken was hanging from a bar in the ceiling. Three of our companions, sweating and out of breath, came back with some bales of straw.

"Make room, you fellows!"

The young fellow of fifteen, for his part, had brought an aluminum saucepan and a frying pan from the abandoned farm.

Were others doing the same in my house?

I can remember some amusing exchanges which made us laugh in spite of ourselves.

"Let's hope he doesn't run the train down the embankment."

"What do you think the rails are for, you idiot?"

"Trains can run off the rails, even in peacetime, can't they? So which of us two is the idiot?"

A group of people went on fussing around the engine for some time, and it came as a surprise to hear it whistle in the end like an ordinary train. We moved off slowly, almost at a walking pace, without any jolting, before gradually picking up speed.

Ten minutes later we passed a road which crossed the line and which was crowded with carts and cattle, with cars here and there trying to get through. Two or three peasants waved to us, more solemn and serious than we were, and it seemed to me that they looked at us enviously.

Later on, we saw a road which ran parallel with the line for some time, with army trucks driving in both directions and spluttering motorcycles weaving in and out.

I imagine, although I didn't make sure afterward, that it was the road from Aumagne to Rethel. In any case, we were getting near to Rethel, judging by the increasing number of signals and houses, the sort of houses you find around towns.

"Do you come from Belgium?"

I couldn't think of anything else to say to Anna, who was sitting beside me on the trunk.

"From Namur. They suddenly decided, in the middle

of the night, to set us free. We'd have had to wait until the morning to get our things, because nobody had the key to the place where they're locked up. I preferred to run to the station and jump on the first train."

I didn't bat an eyelid. Perhaps, in spite of myself, I looked surprised, since she added:

"I was in the women's prison."

I didn't ask what for. It struck me almost as natural. In any case, it was no more extraordinary than for me to be there in a cattle car and my wife and daughter on another train, or to have the driver killed on the footplate and, somewhere else, an old man wounded by a bottle which a machine-gun bullet had shattered in his hand. Everything was natural now.

"Are you from Fumay?"

"Yes."

"That was your daughter, was it?"

"Yes. My wife is seven and a half months pregnant."

"You'll find her at Rethel."

"Perhaps."

The others, who had been in the army and were more practical than I was, spread the straw on the floor in readiness for the coming night. It formed a sort of huge communal bed. Some were already lying down on it. The card players kept passing around a bottle of brandy which never left their corner.

We drew into Rethel and there, all of a sudden, for the first time, we became aware that we weren't ordinary people like the rest, but refugees. I say we, although none of my companions confided in me. All the same I think that in that short space of time we had come to react more or less in the same way.

It was the same sort of weariness, for instance, which could be seen on every face, a weariness very different from that which you feel after a sleepless night or a night's work.

Perhaps we hadn't quite reached a state of indifference, but each of us had given up thinking for himself.

Thinking about what, anyway? We knew absolutely nothing. What was happening was beyond us and it was no use thinking or arguing.

For heaven knows how many miles, for instance, I puzzled over the question of the stations. The little stations, the stops, as I have already said, were empty, without even a railwayman to rush out with his whistle and his red flag when the train appeared. On the other hand the bigger stations were packed with people, and police cordons had to be established on the platforms.

I finally hit on an explanation which seems to me to be the right one: namely, that the slow trains had been withdrawn.

The same was true of the roads, the empty ones probably having been closed to traffic for military reasons.

Somebody from Fumay, whom I didn't know, told me, that very morning, when I was sitting beside Anna, that there was a plan for the evacuation of the town and that he had seen a poster about it at the town hall.

"Special trains have been arranged to take refugees to reception centers in the country where everything is ready to accommodate them."

That may be true. I didn't see the poster. I rarely set foot in the town hall, and when we got to the station my wife, Sophie, and I jumped on the first train we saw.

What made me think that my neighbor was right was

that at Rethel nurses, boy scouts, and a whole reception service were waiting for us. There were some stretchers ready, as if somebody already knew what had happened to us, but I learned a little later that our train wasn't the first to have been machine-gunned on the way.

"And our wives? Our kids?" the man with the pipe started shouting, even before the train had come to a stop.

"Where do you come from?" asked an elderly lady in white, who obviously belonged to the upper class.

"Fumay."

I counted at least four trains in the station. There were crowds of people in the waiting rooms and behind the barriers, for barriers had been put up as for an official procession. The place was swarming with soldiers and officers.

"Where are the wounded?"

"But what about my wife, dammit?"

"She may have been on the train which has been sent to Rheims."

"When?"

The more gently the lady in white spoke to him, the more fierce and aggressive he was—on purpose, for he was beginning to feel that he had certain rights.

"About an hour ago."

"They could have waited for us, couldn't they?"

Tears came into his eyes, for he was worried in spite of everything and perhaps he wanted to feel unhappy. That didn't prevent him, a few moments later, from falling on the sandwiches some girls were passing in big baskets from car to car.

"How many can we take?"

"As many as you like. It's useless hoarding them. You'll find fresh sandwiches at the next station."

We were given bowls of hot coffee. A nurse went by asking:

"Nobody sick or wounded?"

Feeding bottles were ready and an ambulance was waiting at the end of the platform. On the next line a train full of Flemings seemed to be on the point of pulling out. They had had their sandwiches and watched us inquisitively as we ate ours.

The Van Straetens are Flemish in origin; they settled at Fumay three generations ago and no longer speak their original language. In the slate-pits, though, they still call my father-in-law the Fleming.

"Take your seats! Watch out for the doors!"

So far they had kept us for hours in stations or sidings. Now they were dealing with us as quickly as possible, as if they were in a hurry to get rid of us.

Because there were too many people on the platform, I couldn't make out the headlines of the newspapers on the bookstall. I only know that there was one in bold lettering with the word "troops."

We were moving and a girl wearing an arm band was running alongside the train to distribute her last bars of chocolate. She threw a handful in our direction. I managed to catch one for Anna.

We were going to find similar reception centers at Rheims and elsewhere. The horse dealer had returned to his place in our car after being allowed to wash in the station lavatories, and he was treated as a hero. I heard Julie call him Jeff. He was holding a bottle of Cointreau which he had bought in the refreshment room along with two oranges whose scent spread throughout the car.

It was between Rethel and Rheims, toward the end of

the afternoon, for we were not moving fast, that a country-woman stood up grumbling:

"I can't help it. I'm not going to make myself ill."

Going over to the open door, she put a cardboard box on the floor, squatted down and relieved herself, still muttering between her teeth.

That too was significant. The conventions were giving way—in any case those which had been in force the day before. Today nobody protested at the sight of the horse dealer dozing with his head on Julie's plump belly.

"You haven't got a cigarette, have you?" Anna asked me.

"I don't smoke."

It had been forbidden in the sanatorium and afterward I hadn't been tempted to take it up. My neighbor passed her one. I hadn't any matches on me either, and because of the straw it worried me to see her smoke, although other people had been smoking since the previous day. Perhaps it was a sort of jealousy on my part, a feeling of displeasure which I can't explain.

We spent a long time in a suburb of Rheims, looking at the backs of the houses, and in the station we were told that our train would be leaving in half an hour.

There was a rush toward the refreshment room, the lavatories, and the inquiry office, where nobody had heard of women, children, and invalids from a train coming from Fumay.

Trains were going through all the time, troop trains, munitions trains, refugee trains, and I still wonder how it was that there weren't more accidents.

"Perhaps your wife has left a message for you?" Anna suggested.

"Where?"

"Why don't you ask those ladies?"

She pointed to the nurses, the young women of the reception service.

"What name did you say?"

The oldest of the women took a note-pad out of her pocket on which I could see names written by different hands, often in a clumsy script.

"Féron? No. Is she a Belgian?"

"She comes from Fumay, and she's traveling with a little girl of four who's holding a doll dressed in blue in her arms."

I was sure that Sophie hadn't let go of her doll.

"She is seven and a half months pregnant," I went on insistently.

"Then go to the sick room, in case she felt ill."

It was an office which had been converted and which smelled of disinfectant. No. They had treated several pregnant women. One of them had had to be taken straight to the nearest maternity home to have her baby, but she wasn't called Féron and her mother was with her.

"Are you worried?"

"Not really."

I was sure that Jeanne would not leave any message for me. It wasn't in her nature. The idea of bothering one of these distinguished ladies, of writing her name in a notebook, of drawing attention to herself, would never have occurred to her.

"Why do you keep touching your left-hand pocket?"

"Because of my spare pair of glasses. I'm afraid of losing them or breaking them."

We were given some more sandwiches, one orange each, and coffee with as much sugar as we liked. Some people put a few lumps in their pockets.

Noticing a pile of pillows in a corner, I asked if it was possible to hire a couple. The person I asked didn't know, and said that the woman in charge wasn't there, that she wouldn't be back for an hour.

Then, feeling a little awkward, I took two pillows, and when I got back into the car my companions rushed to get the others.

Now that I think of it, I am surprised that during that long day Anna and I should have said scarcely anything to each other. As if by common consent, we stayed together. Even when we separated, at Rheims, to go to the respective lavatories, I found her waiting for me outside the men's.

"I've bought a bar of soap," she announced with childish joy. She smelled of soap, and her hair, which she had moistened before arranging, was still wet.

I could count the number of times I had taken a train before that journey. The first time, at the age of fourteen, when I had to go to Saint-Gervais, I had been given a card with my name, my destination, and a note saying:

"In case of accident or difficulties, please inform Madame Jacques Delmotte, Fumay, Ardennes."

Four years later, when I returned home, aged eighteen, I no longer needed a note of that sort.

After that I never went anywhere except to Mézières, periodically, to see the specialist and have an X-ray examination.

Madame Delmotte was my benefactress, as people called her, and I had ended up by adopting that word too. I can't remember the circumstances in which she came to take an interest in me. It was soon after the First World War and I was not yet eleven.

She must have heard about my mother's disappearance,

my father's behavior, my situation as a virtually abandoned child.

At that time I used to go to the church club, and one Sunday our curate, the Abbé Dubois, told me that a lady had invited me to her house for chocolate the following Thursday.

Like all in Fumay, I knew the name of Delmotte, since the family owns the main slate pits and consequently everybody in the town is more or less dependent on them. Those Delmottes, in my mind, were the employer Delmottes.

Madame Jacques Delmotte, who was then about fifty, was the charity Delmotte.

They were all brothers, sisters, brothers-in-law, or cousins; their fortune had a common origin but they nonetheless formed two distinct clans.

Was Madame Delmotte, as some people claimed, ashamed of her family's hardness? Widowed at an early age, she had made a doctor of her son, and he had been killed at the front.

Since then she had lived with two maidservants in a big stone house where she spent her afternoons on the veranda. From the street you could see her knitting for the old people in the almshouse, in a black dress with a narrow white lace collar. Dainty and pink, she gave off a sugary smell.

It was on the veranda that she gave me chocolate to drink and biscuits to eat while asking me questions about school, my friends, what I wanted to do later on, etc. Making no mention of my mother and father, she asked me if I would like to serve at mass, with the result that I was a choirboy for two years.

She invited me to her house nearly every Thursday and sometimes another little boy or girl shared our snack. We were invariably given homemade biscuits of two sorts, bright yellow ones with lemon flavoring and brown ones with spices and almonds.

I can still remember the smell of the veranda and the warmth in winter, which wasn't the same as anywhere else and struck me as subtler and more pervasive.

Madame Delmotte came to see me when I had what was diagnosed at first as dry pleurisy, and it was she, in her car driven by Désiré, who took me to see a specialist at Mézières.

Three weeks later, thanks to her, I was admitted to a sanatorium where I wouldn't have obtained a bed without her intervention.

It was she too who, when I got married, gave us the silver bowl which stands on the kitchen sideboard. It would look better in a dining room, but we haven't got one.

I think that Madame Delmotte, indirectly, played an important part in my life and, more directly, in my departure from Fumay.

As for her, she had no need to leave, for, having become an old lady, she was already in her flat at Nice, as she was every year at the same season.

Why did I begin thinking about her? For I did think about her, sitting in my cattle car, where it was dark again, feeling Anna's shoulder against mine and wondering whether I dared to take her hand.

Madame Delmotte had made a choirboy of me and Anna had just left prison. I wasn't interested in finding out why she had been sent to prison and for how long.

I suddenly remembered that she had no luggage, no handbag, that when the gates had been opened the authorities hadn't been able to give back their things to the prisoners. So in all probability she hadn't any money on her. And yet, a little earlier, she had told me that she had just bought a bar of soap.

Jeff and Julie, lying side by side, were kissing each other full on the lips and I could make out the scent of their saliva.

"Don't you feel sleepy?"

"What about you?"

"Perhaps we could lie down?"

"Perhaps."

Both of us were forced to bump against our neighbors, and I would have sworn that there were legs and feet all over the place.

"Are you all right?"

"Yes."

"You aren't cold?"

"No."

Behind me, the man I had taken for a horse dealer hoisted himself imperceptibly onto his neighbor, who, as she spread her legs, brushed against my back. We were so close to one another and my senses were so alert that I knew the exact moment of penetration.

Anna too, I would swear to that. Her face touched my cheek, her hair, her parted lips, but she didn't kiss me and I didn't try to kiss her.

Others besides ourselves were still awake and must have known. The movement of the train was shaking us all; after a while the noise of the wheels on the rails became a sort of music.

I am possibly going to express myself crudely, out of clumsiness, precisely because I have always been a prudish man, even in my thoughts.

I wasn't discontented with my way of life. I had chosen

it. I had patiently realized an ideal which, until the previous day—I repeat this in all sincerity—had satisfied me completely.

Now I was there, in the dark, with the song of the train, red and green lights passing by, telegraph wires, other bodies stretched out in the straw, and close beside me, within reach of my hand, what the Abbé Dubois called the carnal act was taking place.

Against my own body, a woman's body pressed itself, tense, vibrant, and a hand moved to pull up the black dress, to push the panties down to the feet which kicked them off with an odd jerking movement.

We still hadn't kissed each other. It was Anna who drew me toward her, on top of her, both of us as silent as snakes.

Julie's breathing grew quicker and louder just as Anna was helping me to enter her, and I suddenly found myself there.

I didn't cry out. But I came close to doing so. I came close to talking incoherently, saying thank you, telling of my happiness, or else complaining, for that happiness hurt me. Hurt me with the attempt to reach the unattainable.

I should have liked to express all at once my affection for this woman whom I hadn't known the day before, but who was a human being, who in my eyes was becoming *the* human being.

I bruised her unconsciously, my hands trying to grasp the whole of her.

"Anna..."

"Hush!"

"I love you."

"Hush!"

For the first time in my life I had said "I love you" like

that, from the depths of my heart. Perhaps it wasn't she that I loved, but life? I don't know how to put it: I was inside her life, and I should have liked to stay there for hours, never to think of anything else, to become like a plant in the sun.

Our lips met, each mouth as moist as the other. I didn't think of asking her, as I used to during my experiences as a young man:

"Can I?"

I could, seeing that she wasn't worried, seeing that she didn't push me away but on the contrary held me inside her.

Finally our lips parted at the same time as our arms and legs relaxed.

"Don't move," she whispered.

And, with both of us invisible to each other, she stroked my forehead gently, following the lines of my face with her hand, like a sculptor.

Still in a whisper, she asked me:

"Did you enjoy that?"

Hadn't I been right in thinking that I had an appointment with Fate?

4

AS USUAL, I WOKE UP AT DAWN, ABOUT HALF past five in the morning. Several of my companions, mostly peasants, were already sitting, wide awake, on the floor of the car. So as not to wake the others, they just said good morning to me with their eyes.

Although one of the sliding doors had been shut for the night, you could feel the biting cold which always precedes sunrise, and, afraid that Anna might catch cold, I spread my jacket over her shoulders and her chest.

So far I hadn't really looked at her. I took advantage of her being asleep to examine her solemnly, somewhat disturbed by what I saw. I was rather inexperienced. Until then I had scarcely seen anybody except my wife and daughter, and I knew how both of them looked in the early morning.

When she wasn't pregnant and oppressed by the weight of her body, Jeanne seemed younger at dawn than she did during the day. With her features erased as it were, she took on the pouting expression of a little girl, roughly the same as Sophie, innocent and satisfied.

Anna was younger than my wife, I put her down as twenty-two, twenty-three at the most, but her face was that of someone much older, as I noticed that morning. I also realized, looking at her more closely, that she was a foreigner.

Not only because she came from another country, I
didn't know which, but because she had a different life, different thoughts, different feelings from the people at Fumay
and all the others I knew.

Instead of letting herself go, to get rid of her weariness,
she had curled up, on the defensive, with a crease in the
middle of her forehead, and now and then the corners of
her mouth twitched as if she felt a pain or experienced a
disagreeable mental picture.

Her flesh didn't look like Jeanne's flesh either. It was
firmer, more solid, with muscles capable of suddenly becoming taut, like those of a cat.

I didn't know where we were. There were poplars lining
meadows and cornfields which were still green. Billboards
kept slipping by as usual, and once we passed close to an
almost deserted road where there was nothing to remind
us of the war.

I had some water in my bottles, a towel, a shaving brush,
and everything I needed in my suitcase; I took the opportunity to have a shave, for I had been ashamed, ever since the
day before, of the reddish hairs, a quarter of an inch long,
which covered my cheeks and my chin.

When I finished, Anna was looking at me, motionless,
and I didn't know how long she had been awake.

She must have taken the opportunity, as I had a little
earlier, to look at me inquisitively. I smiled at her while I
was wiping my face, and she returned my smile, in what
struck me as an embarrassed way, or as if her thoughts were
somewhere else.

I could still see the crease in her forehead. Propping herself up on her elbow, she found my jacket covering her.

"Why did you do that?"

If she hadn't spoken first, I wouldn't have known whether to use the *tu* or the *vous* form of address. Thanks to her, everything became easy.

"Before sunrise it was rather chilly."

She didn't react like Jeanne either. Jeanne would have been profuse in her thanks, would have felt obliged to protest, to show that she was touched.

Anna simply asked me:

"Did you get any sleep?"

"Yes."

She spoke in a low voice, on account of the people who were still asleep, but didn't think it necessary, as I had done, to give a friendly glance to those of our companions who were already awake and who were looking at us.

I wonder whether it wasn't that which, the day before, as soon as she had slipped into our car, had struck me about her. She didn't live with other people. She didn't mix. She remained alone among others.

It may seem ridiculous to say that, after what had happened the previous evening. All the same, I know what I mean. She had followed me along the track when I hadn't called her. I had given her an empty bottle, without asking her for anything in exchange. I hadn't spoken to her. I hadn't asked her any questions.

She had accepted a place on my trunk without feeling the need to say thank you, just as with the jacket now. And, when our bodies had drawn together, she had bared her belly and guided my movements.

"You aren't thirsty?"

There was some water left in the second bottle, and I gave her some in a camping cup which my wife had put in the suitcase.

"What time is it?"

"Ten past six."

"Where are we?"

"I don't know."

She ran her fingers through her hair, still looking at me thoughtfully.

"You're a cool one," she finally concluded, talking to herself. "You always stay cool. Life doesn't frighten you. You haven't any problems, have you?"

"Can't you shut up, the two of you?" grumbled fat Julie.

We smiled and sat down on the trunk to watch the countryside go by. I took her hand. She let me, a little surprised, I think, especially when I raised it to my lips to kiss her fingertips.

A long time afterward, the sight of the congregation coming out of a village church reminded me that it was Sunday, and I was amazed at the thought that, two days before at the same time, I had been at home, wondering whether we ought to leave.

I saw myself again throwing corn to the hens while the water was boiling for my coffee; then I recalled Monsieur Matray's head appearing over the wall, my wife at the window, her face at once drawn and puffy, and later my daughter's anxious voice.

It was as if I could still hear the comical dialogue, on the radio, about the colonel who couldn't be found, and I understood it better now that I was plunged in the muddle myself.

We were moving slowly again. A bend in the line took us nearly all the way around the village, which was perched on a hillock.

The church and the houses weren't the same shape or

the same color as in our part of the world, but the congregation outside the church was behaving in accordance with an identical ritual.

The men in their black clothes, all old because the others were at the front, were standing about in groups, and you could tell that it wouldn't be long before they went into the inn.

The old women were going off one by one, hurrying along and keeping close to the walls, while the girls in bright dresses and the youths stood waiting for one another, holding their missals in their hands, and the children started running immediately.

Anna was still looking at me, and I wondered if she knew what mass on Sunday was like. Before Sophie was born, Jeanne and I used to go to high mass at ten o'clock. Afterward we went for a stroll around the town, greeting our acquaintances, before stopping at her sister's to collect our cake.

I paid for it. I had insisted on paying for it, accepting nothing but a discount of twenty percent. Often the cake was still warm, and on the way home I could smell the sugar on it.

After Sophie, Jeanne got into the habit of going to the seven o'clock mass while I looked after the child, and later, when the little girl could walk, I took her with me to the ten o'clock mass while my wife cooked lunch.

Was there a high mass that morning at Fumay? Were there still enough members of the congregation? Had the Germans bombed or invaded the town?

"What are you thinking about? Your wife?"

"No."

That was true. Jeanne figured only incidentally in these

thoughts. I was thinking just as much about old Monsieur
Matray and the schoolmaster's curly-haired little girl. Had
their car managed to make its way through the chaos on the
roads? Had Monsieur Reversé been to get our hens and our
poor Nestor?

I wasn't upset. I asked myself these questions objectively,
almost playfully, because everything had become possible,
even, for example, the razing of Fumay to the ground and
the shooting of its population.

That was just as plausible as our driver's death in the cab
of his engine, or, in my case, making love in the middle of
forty people with a young woman whom I hadn't known
two days before and who had just come out of prison.

More and more of the others had sat down like us, looking around with vacant eyes, and a few were taking food
out of their luggage. We were getting near a town. On the
billboards I had read some names which were familiar to
me, and when I saw that we were at Auxerre I had to make
an effort to remember the map of France.

I don't know why I had got it into my head that we were
going to go through Paris. We had avoided the capital, probably going by way of Troyes during the night.

Now we found ourselves under the big glass roof of a
station whose atmosphere was different from the one where
we had stopped before.

Here it was a real Sunday morning, a prewar Sunday,
with no reception service, no nurses, no girls wearing arm
bands.

A score of people in all were waiting on the green
benches on the platforms, and the sunshine, filtering
through the dirty panes and reduced to light-dust, gave an
unreal quality to the silence and solitude.

"Hey there, guard, are we going to stay here long?"

The guard looked at the front of the train, then at the clock. I don't know why, for he replied:

"I haven't the faintest idea."

"Have we got time to go to the refreshment room?"

"You've got an hour at least, I should say."

"Where are they taking us? "

He went off shrugging his shoulders, indicating that this question didn't come within his province.

I wonder whether we weren't rather annoyed—I say we on purpose—at not being welcomed, at finding ourselves suddenly left to our own resources. Expressing in his fashion the general feeling, somebody called out:

"So nobody's feeding us anymore?"

As if it had become a right.

Right away, seeing that we were now in a civilized part of the world, I said to Anna:

"Are you coming?"

"Where?"

"To have something to eat."

Our first instinctive action, for all of us, once we were on the platform, where we suddenly had too much room, was to look at our train from one end to the other, and it was a disappointment to find that it was no longer the same train.

Not only had the engine been changed, but, behind the tender, I counted fourteen Belgian carriages, as clean-looking as on ordinary trains.

As for our cattle cars and freight cars, there were only three of them left.

"The swine have cut us in two again!"

The doors opened in front, and the first person to get

out was a huge, athletic priest, who went over to the station-master with an air of authority about him.

They talked together. The stationmaster seemed to be agreeing to something, and afterward the priest spoke to the people who had stayed in the carriage, and helped a nun in a white coif to get down onto the platform.

There were four nuns in all, two of them very young, with baby faces, to help out and line up like schoolchildren about forty old men dressed in identical gray woolen suits.

It was an old people's home which had been evacuated, and we learned later that the train to which we had been joined while we were asleep came from Louvain.

The men were all very old, and more or less infirm. Beards had grown, thick and white, on faces as clear-cut as in old pictures.

The extraordinary thing was their meekness, the indifference which you could read in their eyes. They allowed themselves to be taken to the second-class refreshment room, where they were installed as in a refectory while the priest spoke to the manager.

Once again Anna looked at me. Was it because of the priest and the nuns, because she thought that I was familiar with that world? Or was it because the old men in a line reminded her of prison and a discipline which I didn't know but of which she had experience?

I don't know. We kept darting these brief, probing glances at each other like this, only to resume an impassive expression immediately afterward.

THE LIÈGE FORTS IN GERMAN HANDS.

I read this headline on a newspaper on the stall, and, in smaller letters:

PARACHUTISTS ATTACK ALBERT CANAL.

"What do you want to eat? Do you like croissants?"

She nodded.

"Light coffee?"

"Black. If we've got time, I'd like to tidy up first. Would you mind lending me your comb?"

As we had sat down at a table and all the others had been taken, I didn't dare to get up to follow her. Just as she was going through the glass door, I felt my heart sink, for the idea occurred to me that I might never see her again.

Through the window I could see a quiet square, some taxis on a rank, a hotel, and a little blue-painted bar where the waiter was wiping the tables on the terrace.

There was nothing to stop Anna from going.

"Had any news of your wife and daughter?"

Fernand Leroy was standing in front of me, a bottle of beer in his hand, an ironical look in his eye. I said no, trying not to blush, for I realized that he knew what had happened between Anna and myself.

I have never liked Leroy. The son of a sergeant-major in the cavalry, he used to explain to us at school:

"In the cavalry, a sergeant-major is much more important than a lieutenant or even a captain in any other branch of the army."

He always managed to get other boys punished instead of him and the masters were taken in by his innocent expression, something which didn't prevent him from making faces behind their backs.

I learned, later on, that he had failed his *baccalauréat* twice. His father was dead. His mother worked as a cashier in a movie house. He got a job at Hachette's bookshop and, two or three years later, married the daughter of a rich contractor.

Did he marry her for her money? That's none of my business. It was without any malicious intent that I in turn asked:

"Isn't your wife with you?"

"I thought you knew. We're getting a divorce."

If it hadn't been for him, I should have gone to look for Anna.

Time seemed to drag. My hands were getting moist. I was filled with an impatience I had never known before, which, though much stronger, was comparable only to the feeling which had gripped me the previous Friday, in the station at Fumay, when I was wondering whether we would manage to get away.

A waitress came over and I ordered coffee and croissants for two while Leroy put on his horrible smile again. People like him, I thought to myself, are capable of dirtying everything with a glance, and all the time I was waiting I really hated him.

It was only when he saw Anna pushing open the door that he moved away in the direction of the bar, saying:

"I'll leave the two of you."

Yes, the two of us. We were the two of us again. My face must have shown the joy I felt, for Anna had scarcely sat down opposite me before she murmured:

"Were you afraid I wouldn't come back?"

"Yes."

"Why?"

"I don't know. I suddenly felt lost and I nearly ran after you on the platform."

"I haven't any money."

"And if you'd had some?"

"I wouldn't have gone even then."

She didn't say whether this was because of me, but just asked me for some small change which she took to the woman in charge of the ladies' washrooms.

The old men were eating in silence, as they must have done in the institution. The tables had been put together. The priest was at one end, the oldest of the nuns at the other. It was half past ten in the morning. Presumably to provide two meals in one, or because nobody knew what lay ahead of us, each of them had been given some cheese and a hard-boiled egg.

Some of them, who had no teeth left, were munching with their gums. One of them was dribbling so badly that a nun had tied a paper napkin around his neck and was keeping a close watch on his movements. A good many were red-eyed and had thick blue veins standing out on their hands.

"Don't you want to go and wash up too?"

I not only went to have a wash, but I took a clean shirt out of my suitcase in order to change. My traveling companions were in the washrooms, stripped to the waist, washing, shaving, and combing their wet hair. The roller towel was black and had a doggy smell.

"You know how many fellows had her last night?"

I caught my breath and felt a bar across my chest, something which taught me that I was jealous.

"Three, as well as the fat fellow! I counted them, seeing that I hardly slept a wink because of them. But they had to cough up their twenty francs, just like they did in her pub. Have you ever been in her pub?"

"Once, with my brother-in-law."

"Who's your brother-in-law?"

"You saw him when you got married and when you

registered your kids. He's the clerk in the register office."

"Is he here?"

"They aren't allowed to leave. That's what they say, anyway. All the same, I saw with my own eyes a police officer scramming on his motor-bike with his wife up behind him."

Why had I felt frightened? It was all the more ridiculous in that I am a light sleeper and Anna had so to speak slept in my arms.

I also discovered, there in the washrooms, that there had been other couplings during the night, in the corner opposite ours, including some with a huge countrywoman who was over fifty. They even said that old Jules, after a few others had had her, had tried his luck and that she had been hard put to it to push him away.

Wasn't it odd that nobody had made the slightest approach to Anna? They had seen her get on the train by herself, so they knew that she wasn't with me, that we had met by chance. There was no reason, in the minds of those men, why I should enjoy an exclusive privilege.

Yet they just looked at her from a distance. It was true—and that struck me now—that nobody had spoken to her. Had they recognized that she belonged to another race? Did they distrust her?

I rejoined her. The stationmaster came along twice to have a chat with the priest. In that way, as long as the old men stayed at the table, we were in no danger of seeing the train leave without us.

"Do you know where we're going?"

It was the man with the pipe who had suddenly reappeared, clean-shaven, his pockets stuffed with packets of tobacco, of which he had bought a whole stock.

"For the moment my instructions are to send you on

to Bourges, via Clamecy, but all that may change from one minute to the next."

"And after that?"

"They'll decide at Bourges."

"Are we allowed to get off when we like?"

"You want to leave the train?"

"I don't. But there are some people who might like the idea."

"I don't see how they could be prevented, nor why anybody should prevent them."

"Back there they stopped us from leaving the train."

The stationmaster scratched his head and gave serious thought to the question.

"It depends whether you're regarded as evacuees or refugees."

"What's the difference?"

"Were you forced to leave, in a group?"

"No."

"In that case, you're refugees. Did you pay for your ticket?"

"There was nobody in the ticket office."

"Theoretically…"

It was getting too complicated for him, and with an evasive gesture he rushed off in the direction of Platform 3, where a train was due, a real train, with ordinary passengers who knew where they were going and had paid for their tickets.

"You heard what he said?"

I nodded.

"If only I knew where I could find my wife and kids! Back there, they treat you like soldiers or prisoners of war: do this, do that, don't get out on the platform. They give you an orange juice and sandwiches, the women up in front, the men at the back, shoved together like cattle. They cut the train in two without telling you, they machine-gun you, they separate you—in fact, you aren't human beings anymore.

"And then here, all of a sudden, you've got complete freedom. Do what you like! Go and jump in the river if you feel like it…"

Perhaps the next day, or that evening, the station at Auxerre would be different. My favorite memory, seeing that we had enough time, is of walking about outside with Anna. It seemed so wonderful to be in a real square, walking on real pavingstones, among people who weren't worried yet about planes.

We saw groups of people slowly making their way home from church, and we went into the little blue-painted bar where I drank a lemonade while Anna, after a furtive glance, ordered an Italian apéritif.

It was the first station since we had left which we had seen from the outside, with its big clock and its frosted-glass porch, the shadowy entrance hall contrasting with the sunny square and the multicolored magazines all around the kiosk.

"Where do you come from, you two?"

"Fumay."

"I thought that was a Belgian train."

"There are Belgian carriages and French carriages."

"Last night we had some Dutch people. It seems they're being taken to Toulouse. What about you?"

"We don't know."

The waiter raised his head and looked at me incredulously. It was only later that I understood his reaction.

"What, you don't know? You mean you just let them trundle you around wherever they like?"

Some towns had entered the war, while others hadn't as yet. Because that was so, we had seen from the train quiet villages where everyone was going about their business and little towns invaded by convoys.

It didn't depend entirely on how close the front was. Indeed, was there such a thing as a front?

At Bourges, for instance, in the middle of the afternoon, we found a reception service as in the north, a platform swarming with families waiting among suitcases and bundles.

They were Belgians again. I wondered how they could have arrived before us. They must have traveled along another line, not as busy as ours, but they had had a similar experience, only more serious, near the frontier.

Several planes had machine-gunned them. Everybody had got out—men, women, and children—to lie down in the ditch. The Germans had returned to the attack twice, putting the engine out of action and killing or wounding a dozen people.

We were forbidden to leave the train so that we shouldn't get mixed up, but conversations started with the people on the platform while we were being given something to eat and drink.

At Auxerre I had bought a couple of packed meals. We took the sandwiches all the same and put them aside, for we were becoming cautious.

The Belgians on the platform were dazed and gloomy. They had walked for two hours on the pebbles and sleepers along the track before reaching a station, carrying what they could, but leaving most of their things behind.

As usual, the man with the pipe was the best informed of us all, first because of his strategic position near the door, and then because he was not afraid of asking questions.

"You see that blonde over there in a dress with blue dots? She carried her dead child all the way to the station. It seems it was a very small place. Everybody came to see them and she gave the baby to the mayor, who's a farmer by trade, to be buried."

She was eating absent-mindedly, with a vacant look in her eyes, sitting on a brown suitcase tied up with ropes.

"A train went to pick them up and left the dead and wounded at a bigger station, they don't know which. Here, they made them get off their train because they needed the carriages, and they've been waiting since eight o'clock this morning."

They, too, looked at us enviously, without understanding what was happening to them. A pretty, fresh-faced nurse, without a single mark on her starched uniform, was feeding a baby from a bottle while the mother was hunting through her luggage for some clean diapers.

We didn't see their train come in, so I don't know when they managed to leave, or where they were taken in the end. It's true that I didn't know where my wife and daughter were either.

I tried to find out, and asked the woman who seemed to be in charge of the reception service. She answered calmly:

"Don't worry. Everything has been provided for. There will be lists printed."

"Where shall I be able to see these lists?"

"At the reception center you're going to. You're Belgian, aren't you?"

"No. I'm from Fumay."

"Then what are you doing on a Belgian train?"

I heard that question ten, twenty times. People came close to resenting our presence on the train. Our three wretched cars, as the result of heaven knows what mistake, weren't where they ought to have been, and we narrowly missed getting the blame.

"Where are they sending the Belgians?"

"As a general rule, to Gironde and the Charente departments."

"Is this train going there?"

Like the stationmaster at Auxerre, she preferred to answer with a vague gesture.

Contrary to what you might imagine, I thought of Jeanne and my daughter without overmuch anxiety, indeed with a certain serenity.

Once, my heart had missed a beat, when I had heard about the train which had been machine-gunned and the dead child which its mother had been obliged to leave at a little station.

Then I had told myself that that had happened in the north, that Jeanne's train had been ahead of ours and had therefore crossed the danger zone before us.

I loved my wife. She was just as I had wanted her and had brought me exactly what I expected from my partner in life. I had no complaints to make of her. I wasn't looking for any either, and that was why I resented Leroy's ambiguous smile so keenly.

Jeanne had nothing to do with what was happening now, any more than the ten o'clock mass, for instance, my sister-in-law's confectionery business, or the labeled radios on the shelves in my workshop.

I sometimes say "we" when talking of the people in our

train because, on certain points, I know that our reactions were the same. But on this point I speak for myself, although I am convinced that I wasn't the only one in my position.

A break had occurred. That didn't mean that the past had ceased to exist, still less that I repudiated my family and had stopped loving them.

It was just that, for an indeterminate period, I was living on another level, where the values had nothing in common with those of my previous existence.

I might say that I was living on two levels at once, but that for the moment the one which counted was the new one, represented by our car with its smell of the stables, by faces I hadn't known a few days before, by the baskets of sandwiches carried by the young ladies with the arm bands, and by Anna.

I am convinced that she understood me. She no longer tried to cheer me up by telling me, for instance, that my wife and daughter were in no danger and that I would soon find them again.

Something she had said that morning came back to me. "You're a cool one."

She took me for a strong-minded character, and I suspect that that is why she attached herself to me. At that time I knew nothing of her life, apart from the reference she had made to the Namur prison, and I know little more now. It is obvious that she had no ties, nothing solid to lean on.

But, in fact, wasn't she the stronger of the two of us?

At the Blois station, unless I am mistaken, where another reception service was waiting for us, she was the first to ask:

"There hasn't been a train here from Fumay, has there?"

"Where's Fumay?"

"In the Ardennes, near the Belgian frontier."

"Oh, we've had so many Belgians going through!"

On the roads, too, we could now see Belgian cars following one another bumper to bumper, in two lines, so that jams occurred everywhere. There were also some French cars, but far fewer, mainly from the northern departments.

I didn't know the Loire, which was sparkling in the sunshine, and we caught sight of two or three historic chateaux which were familiar to me from picture postcards.

"Have you been here before?" I asked Anna.

She hesitated before answering "yes" and squeezing the tips of my fingers. Did she guess that she was hurting me a little, that I would have preferred her not to have a past?

It was absurd. But hadn't everything become absurd and wasn't this what I had been looking for?

The horse dealer was asleep. Fat Julie had drunk too much and was holding her bosom in both hands, looking at the door with the expression of somebody who expects to be sick any minute.

There were bottles and scraps of food all over the straw, and the fifteen-year-old boy had found a couple of army blankets somewhere.

Everybody had his special place, his corner which he was sure of finding again after getting down onto the platform when we were allowed to leave the train.

It seemed to me that there were fewer of us than at the beginning of our journey, that four or five people were missing, but, not having counted them, I couldn't be sure, except about the little girl whom the nuns, seeing her with us, had taken off to their carriage as if we were devils.

At Tours, that evening, we were given big bowls of soup, with pieces of boiled beef and some bread. Night was beginning to fall. I was impatient to rediscover our intimacy of the previous night. I must have shown it, for Anna looked at me with a certain tenderness.

The latest news was that we were being taken to Nantes, where our final destination would be decided on.

Wrapping himself up in a blanket, somebody called out:

"Good night, everybody!"

A few cigarettes were still glowing, and I waited, motionless, my eyes fixed on the signals which I kept confusing with the stars.

Jeff was still asleep. All the same there were some furtive movements near Julie until her voice suddenly broke the silence:

"No, boys! Tonight I want a bit of shut-eye. You'd better get that into your heads."

Anna laughed in my ear and we waited another half hour.

5

ONE OF THE OLD MEN FROM THE INFIRMARY died during the night. I don't know which, for he was taken off at Nantes in the morning, his face covered with a towel. The Belgian consul was waiting on the platform and the priest went into the stationmaster's office with him for the formalities.

The reception service here was bigger than before, not only in the number of ladies with arm bands, but because there seemed to be some people concerned with organizing the movements of refugees.

I hoped that I was at last going to see the sea, for the first time in my life. I gathered that it was a long way off, that we were in an estuary, but I caught sight of some ships' masts and funnels, I heard some hooters, and near to us a whole trainful of bluejackets alighted: they lined up on the platform and marched out of the station.

The weather was as unbelievably glorious as it had been on the previous days, and we were able to wash and have breakfast before leaving.

I had a moment's anxiety when an assistant stationmaster started talking to somebody who looked like an official, pointing to our three shabby cars, as if there were some question of uncoupling them.

It was becoming increasingly obvious that, incorporated in the Belgian train through no fault of ours, we presented a problem, but finally we were allowed to go.

Our biggest surprise was fat Julie. A few moments before the whistle blew, she appeared on the platform, radiant, fresh-complexioned, wearing a floral cotton dress without a single crease in it.

"What do you think Julie's been doing, boys, while you've been wallowing in the straw? She's been and had a bath, a real hot bath, in the hotel opposite. And on top of that she's managed to buy herself a dress on the way!"

We were traveling down toward the Vendée, where, an hour later, I caught a glimpse of the sea in the distance. Deeply stirred, I reached for Anna's hand. I had seen the sea at the movies and in colored photos, but I hadn't imagined that it was so bright or so huge and insubstantial.

The water was the same color as the sky, and, since it was reflecting the light, since the sun was both up above and down below, there was no longer any limit to anything and the word "infinite" sprang to my mind.

Anna understood that it was a new experience for me. She smiled. We were both of us lighthearted. The whole car was gay all day.

We now knew more or less what was waiting for us, for the consul had visited the first carriages to cheer up his fellow countrymen, and the man with the pipe, always on the watch, had brought us the news.

"It seems that the Belgians' destination is La Rochelle. That's their marshaling yard, so to speak. They've set up a sort of camp there with huts, beds, and everything."

"And what about us? Seeing that we aren't Belgians?"

"Oh, we'll manage."

We were moving slowly and I kept reading place names which reminded me of books I had read: Pornic, Saint-Jean-de-Monts, Croix-de-Vie…

We caught sight of the Île d'Yeu, which, in the dazzling sunlight, you might have taken for a cloud stretched out on a level with the water.

For hours our train seemed to be taking the longest route, as if we were on an excursion, going off on side tracks to stop in the open country and then coming back again.

We were no longer afraid of getting off and jumping on again, for we knew that the engineer would wait for us.

I realized why we were following such a circuitous route, and also perhaps why we had taken such a long time coming from the Ardennes.

The regular trains, with normal passengers who paid for their tickets, were still running, and on the main lines there was also a continual traffic of troop trains and munitions trains which had priority over the rest.

In nearly every station, as well as the ordinary staff, we started seeing an officer giving orders.

As we belonged to none of these categories, we kept being shunted into a siding to make room.

Once I overheard a telephone conversation in a pretty station red with geraniums, where a dog was stretched out across the doorway of the stationmaster's office. The stationmaster, who was feeling hot, had pushed his cap back and was toying with his flag, which was lying on the desk.

"Is that you, Dambois?"

Another stationmaster explained to me that this wasn't an ordinary telephone. If I remember rightly, it is called the block telephone and you can only speak to and hear the

nearest station on it. That is how notice of a train's approach
is given.

"How are things with you?"

There were some hens behind some chicken wire, just
like at home, and a well-kept garden. The stationmaster's
wife was doing the rooms upstairs and came to the window
now and then to shake her duster.

"I've got the 237 here... I can't keep them much longer,
because I'm expecting the 161... Is your siding free?... Is
Hortense's café open?... Tell her she's going to have a crowd
of customers... Right!... Thanks... I'll send it on to you..."

The result was that we spent three hours in a tiny station next to an inn painted pink. The tables were taken by
storm. Everybody drank. Everybody ate. Anna and I stayed
outside, under a pine tree, and at times we felt embarrassed
at having nothing to say to each other.

If I had to describe the place, I could only talk of the
patches of sunshine and shadow, of the pink daylight, of the
green vines and currant bushes, of my feeling of torpor and
animal well-being, and I wonder whether, that particular
day, I didn't get as close as possible to perfect happiness.

Smells existed as they had in my childhood, the quiver-
ing of the air, the imperceptible noises of life. I think I have
said this before, but as I am not writing all at one go but
scribbling a few lines here, a page or two there, in secret, on
the sly, I am bound to repeat myself.

When I began my story, I was tempted to start with a
foreword, for sentimental rather than practical reasons. You
see, at the sanatorium the library consisted mainly of books
dating back before 1900, and it was the fashion for authors
in the last century to write a foreword, an introduction, or
a preface.

The paper in those books, yellow and speckled with brown spots, was thicker and shinier than in present-day books, and they had a pleasant smell which, for me, has clung to the characters in the novels. The black cloth of the bindings was as shiny as the elbows of an old jacket, and I found the same cloth again in the public library at Fumay.

I dropped the idea of a foreword for fear of seeming conceited. It is true that I may repeat myself, get mixed up, even contradict myself, for I am writing this mainly in the hope of discovering a certain truth.

As for the events which don't concern me personally, I record them, when I witnessed them, to the best of my recollection. To find certain dates I would have had to look up the back numbers of the newspapers, and I don't know where to find them.

I am sure about the date of Friday the 10th, which must be in the history books now. I am sure too, more or less, about the itinerary we followed, although, even on the train, some of my companions started mentioning names of stations which we hadn't seen.

A road which was deserted in the morning, in those days, could be swarming with life an hour later. Everything went terribly fast and terribly slowly. People were still talking about fighting in Holland when the Panzers had already reached Sedan.

Again, my memory may occasionally play tricks on me. As I said about the last morning at Fumay, I could reconstruct certain hours minute by minute, whereas with others I can only remember the general atmosphere.

It was like that on the train, especially with the fatigue, the dull, dazed feeling which resulted from our way of life.

We no longer had any responsibilities, any decisions to make. Nothing depended on us, not even our own fate.

One detail, for instance, has worried me a lot, because I am rather persnickety and tend to think over an idea for hours until I have got it right. When I wrote about the plane machine-gunning our train, about the fireman gesticulating beside his engine, and about the dead driver, I didn't mention the guard. Yet there ought to have been a guard, whose job it was to make the necessary decisions.

I didn't see him. Did he exist or didn't he? Once again, things didn't necessarily happen in a logical way.

As for the Vendée, I know that my skin, my eyes, the whole of my body have never drunk in the sunshine as greedily as they did that day, and I can say for sure that I appreciated every nuance of the light, every shade of green of the meadows, the fields, and the trees.

A cow, stretched out in the shade of an oak, all white and brown, its wet muzzle twitching endlessly, ceased to be a familiar animal, a commonplace sight, to become...

To become what? I can't find the words I want. I am no good at expressing myself. The fact remains that tears came into my eyes looking at a cow. And, that day on the terrace of a pink-painted inn, my eyes remained for a long time fixed in wonderment on a fly circling around a drop of lemonade.

Anna noticed. I became aware that she was smiling. I asked her why.

"I've just seen you as you must have been when you were five."

Even the smells of the human body, particularly that of sweat, were pleasant to rediscover. Finally, I had found a part of the world where the land was on a level with the sea and where you could see as many as five church steeples at once.

The country people went about their work as usual, and when our train stopped they just looked at it from a distance, without feeling the need to come and inspect us or ask us questions.

I noticed that there were far more geese and ducks than there were at home, and that the houses were so low that you could touch the roofs, as if the inhabitants were afraid of the wind carrying them away.

I saw Luçon, which made me think of Cardinal Richelieu, then Fontenay-le-Comte. We could have arrived at La Rochelle in the evening, but the stationmaster at Fontenay came and explained to us that it would be difficult to disembark us in the dark and install us in the reception center.

You have to remember that, on account of the air raids, the gas lamps and all the other street lights were painted blue and people had to hang black curtains in their windows, so that at night, in the towns, the passersby carried flashlights and the cars drove at a walking pace, with just their side lights on.

"They're going to find you a quiet spot to spend the night in. And somebody'll bring you food and drink."

It was true. We approached the sea only to leave it behind again, and our train, which had no timetable to observe and seemed to be looking for a resting place, ended up by stopping in a meadow, near to a way station.

It was six o'clock in the evening. You couldn't feel the chill of twilight yet. Nearly everybody got out to stretch their legs, except for the old men in the care of the priest and the nuns, and I saw middle-aged women with grim faces bending down to pick daisies and buttercups.

Somebody said the old men in the coarse gray uniforms were mental patients. That may have been the case. At La Rochelle they were met by nurses and more nuns who piled them into a couple of coaches.

I had already had an idea, and I went over to Dédé, the fifteen-year-old boy, to buy one of his blankets from him. It was more difficult than I had expected. He haggled more stubbornly than a peasant at a fair, but I got my way in the end.

Anna watched us with a smile, unable, I imagine, to guess the object of our bargaining.

I was enjoying myself. I felt young. Or rather I didn't feel any age in particular.

"What were you talking about so earnestly?"

"An idea of mine."

"I know what it is."

"I doubt it."

"Bet you I do."

As if I were a boy and she were a little girl.

"Tell me what you're thinking, to see if you've guessed."

"You don't want to sleep on the train."

It was true, and I was surprised that she had thought of it. To my mind, it was a rather crazy idea, which couldn't occur to anybody but myself. I had never had an opportunity to sleep in the open air as a child because my mother wouldn't have allowed it, and besides it would have been difficult in a town, and later on account of my illness.

As soon as the stationmaster had spoken of finding us a quiet spot in the country, the idea had occurred to me, and now I had got hold of a blanket which would protect us from the dew and safeguard our intimacy.

A yellow car arrived with a jovial nurse and four boy

scouts of sixteen or seventeen. They brought us sandwiches, bars of chocolate, and a couple of cans of hot coffee. They also had some blankets, which were reserved for the children and the old men.

The doors banged. For a good hour, in the slowly fading light, there was a confused hubbub in which cries in Flemish could be heard the loudest.

If it hadn't been for that night's halt, I would never have known that there were some babies in the Belgian carriages. But the nurse knew, thanks to the block telephone, and she had brought along some feeding bottles and a big bundle of diapers.

That was of no interest to our car. Not because they were Belgians but because the children didn't belong to our group. Besides, the French people in the other two freight cars, although they had got on the train at the same time as us at Fumay, were just as foreign to us.

Cells had been formed, airtight, self-contained. And in each cell smaller cells could be observed, such as the card players or the couple consisting of Anna and myself.

Frogs started croaking, and new sounds could be heard in the meadows and the trees.

We went for a stroll without holding hands, without touching each other, and Anna smoked one of the cigarettes I had bought her at Nantes.

The idea of talking about love never occurred to us, and I wonder today if it was really love that we felt for each other. I mean love in the sense which is usually given to the word, for to my mind it was much more.

She didn't know what I did for a living and showed no desire to find out. She knew that I had had tuberculosis, for I had happened to remark, on the subject of sleep:

"At the sanatorium they used to turn the lights out at eight o'clock."

She looked at me immediately and that movement was characteristic of her, as was her glance which I would find difficult to describe. It was as if an idea had struck her all of a sudden, not an idea born of reflection, but something palpable if fleeting which she had caught instinctively in flight.

"Now I understand," she murmured.

"You understand what?"

"You."

"What have you found out?"

"That you've spent several years shut up."

I didn't press the point but I think that I understood in my turn. She had been shut up, too. The name of the place where you are condemned to live between four walls is of small importance.

Didn't she mean that it leaves a mark, and that she had recognized that mark in me without knowing how to explain it?

We walked slowly back to the darkened train where nothing could be seen but the firefly glimmer of cigarettes and we could hear a few voices whispering.

I collected the blanket. We looked for a place, our place, some soft earth, some tall grass, a gentle slope.

A clump of three trees hid us from sight and there was also a big, smelly patch of cow dung in which somebody had walked. The moon wouldn't rise before three o'clock in the morning.

We stood for a while rather awkwardly facing one another, and to keep my composure I started arranging the blanket.

I remember Anna throwing away her cigarette, which

went on glowing in the grass, taking off her dress with a movement I hadn't seen before, and then removing her underclothes.

She came up to me then, naked, surprised by the cold which made her shiver once or twice, and gently pulled me down on the ground.

I realized right away that she wanted it to be my night. She had guessed that I was looking forward to it, just as she had guessed so many of my thoughts.

It was she who took the initiative all the time; she too who pushed away the blanket so that our bodies should be in contact with the ground, with the smell of the earth and the grass.

When the moon rose, I was still awake. Anna had put her dress on again and we were rolled up in the blanket, pressed against each other, on account of the cool of the night.

I could see her dark hair with its glints of red, her exotic profile, and her pale skin whose texture was unlike anything I had ever known before.

We had blended so closely into each other that we had only a single smell.

I don't know what I thought about while I was looking at her. I was in a serious mood, neither gay nor sad. The future didn't worry me. I refused to let it intervene in the present.

I suddenly noticed that, for the past twenty-four hours, I hadn't worried once about my spare pair of glasses, which were probably lying somewhere in the meadow or in the straw in our car.

Every now and then her body was shaken by a shudder and the crease in her forehead deepened, as if at a bad dream or in a spasm of pain.

I finally dropped off to sleep. Instead of waking up of my

own accord, as I usually did, I was roused from sleep by the sound of footsteps. Somebody was walking close to us, the man with the pipe, whom I called the concierge. A whiff of his tobacco, unexpected in that country dawn, came to my nostrils.

He was an early riser like me, and doubtless something of a hermit, in spite of his wife and children for whom he kept clamoring with exaggerated ill humor. He was walking with the same steps that I used to walk with in my garden in the morning, and our eyes met.

I thought he had a kindly look about him. With his sloping shoulders and his lopsided nose, he looked like a friendly gnome in a picture book.

Anna woke up with a start.

"Is it time to go?"

"I don't think so. The sun hasn't risen yet."

A slight mist was rising from the ground and some cows were lowing in a distant barn from which a gleam of light was filtering. Somebody was presumably milking them.

The day before, we had noticed a tap behind the brick shelter at the way station. We went there to clean ourselves up. There was nobody around.

"Hold the blanket."

Anna undressed in a flash and dashed some icy water over her body.

"Go and get my soap, will you? It's in the straw, behind your trunk."

Once she had dried herself and got dressed again, she said:

"Your turn!"

I hesitated.

"They're beginning to get up," I objected.

"What about it? Even if they see you stark naked?"

I followed her example, my lips blue with cold, and she rubbed my back and chest with the towel.

The yellow car returned, bringing back the same nurse and the same scouts, who looked like overgrown children or unfinished men.

They brought us more coffee, some bread and butter, and feeding bottles for the babies.

I know nothing of what happened on the train that night, nor whether it is true, as rumor had it, that a woman gave birth to a child. I find that hard to believe, for I didn't hear anything.

They treated us like schoolchildren on holiday, and the nurse, although she was under forty, ordered us about like an infants' class.

"Heavens above, what a smell of dirty feet! When you get to the camp, you'll have to have a good wash, all of you. And you, Grandpa, did you empty all those bottles by yourself?"

She spotted Julie.

"Hey, Fatty, what are you waiting for? Are you having a lie-in this morning? Get a move on! An hour from now, you'll be at La Rochelle."

There, at last, the sea was close to us, the port adjoining the station, with steamers on one side, and on the other side fishing boats whose sails and nets were drying in the sun.

I took possession of the scene immediately and let it get right under my skin. If there were several trains on the tracks I didn't pay any attention to them, and I didn't see anything at all. I didn't pay any attention either to the more or less important individuals who came and went, giving orders, girls in white, soldiers, boy scouts.

The old men were helped out of the train and the priest

counted them as if he were afraid of losing or forgetting some.

"Everybody over to the reception center, opposite the station."

I picked up my trunk and the suitcase which Anna had tried to take out of my hands, leaving her nothing to carry but the blanket and our empty bottles, which might come in useful again.

Some armed soldiers watched us pass and turned around to look at Anna, who was following close behind me, as if she suddenly felt lost and frightened.

I didn't understand why until a little later. Outside, the scouts pointed to the deal huts which had been put up in a public park, only a few feet from the dock. There was a smaller hut, hardly any bigger than a newspaper kiosk, which was being used as an office, and we found ourselves queuing with the others outside the open door.

Our group had broken up. We were mixed up with the Belgians, who were the bigger party, and we had no idea what was going to happen to us.

From a distance we witnessed the loading of the old men into the coaches. A couple of ambulances drove away too. The towers of the town could be seen some way off, and some refugees who were already installed in the camp came and looked at us inquisitively. A lot of them were Flemings and were delighted to find some fellow countrymen.

One of them, who spoke French, asked me with a pronounced accent:

"Where do you come from?"

"Fumay."

"Then you shouldn't be here, should you? This is a camp for Belgians."

We exchanged anxious glances, Anna and I, while we waited our turn in the sun.

"Have your identity cards ready."

I hadn't got one, because at that time they were not compulsory in France. I hadn't a passport either, never having been abroad.

I saw some of the people coming out of the office go over to the huts, while others were sent to wait on the pavement, probably for transport to take them somewhere else.

Getting closer to the door, I overheard some snatches of conversation.

"What's your trade, Peeters?"

"I'm a fitter, but since the war..."

"Do you want a job?"

"I'm not a slacker, you know."

"Have you got a wife, children?"

"My wife's over there, the one in the green dress, with the three kids."

"You can start work tomorrow at the factory at Aytré, and you'll get the same wage as the French. Go and wait on the pavement. You'll be taken to Aytré, where they'll find you lodgings."

"You mean that?"

"Next."

Next came old Jules, who, one of the last to arrive, had slipped into the queue.

"Your identity card."

"I haven't got one."

"You've lost it?"

"I've never had one."

"You're Belgian, aren't you?"

"French."

"Then what are you doing here?"

"I'm waiting for you to tell me."

The man spoke in a low voice to somebody I couldn't see.

"Have you any money?"

"Not enough to buy myself a drink."

"You haven't any relatives at La Rochelle?"

"I haven't any relatives anywhere. I'm an orphan from birth."

"We'll see about you later. Go and have a rest."

I could feel Anna getting more and more nervous. I was the second Frenchman to come forward.

"Identity card."

"I'm French."

The man looked at me, irritated.

"Are many of you on the train French?"

"Three cars full."

"Who's been looking after you?"

"Nobody."

"What are you thinking of doing?"

"I don't know."

He nodded toward Anna.

"Is she your wife?"

I hesitated only a second before saying "yes."

"Settle down in the camp for the moment. I don't know what to do about you. This wasn't expected."

Three of the huts were new and roomy, with two rows of mattresses on bails. A few people were still lying down, possibly because they were ill or because they had arrived during the night.

Farther on, an old circus tent made of coarse green canvas had been put up, and they had simply strewn some straw on the ground.

It was there that we put our things down in a corner, Anna and I. People were just beginning to move into the camp. There were a lot of empty spaces. I could see that that wasn't going to last and thought that we would be more likely to be left in peace in the tent than in the huts.

In a smaller, rather shabby tent, some women were busy peeling potatoes and cleaning whole bucketfuls of vegetables.

"Thank you," murmured Anna.

"Why?"

"For what you said."

"I was afraid they might not let you in."

"What would you have done?"

"I'd have gone with you."

"Where?"

"That doesn't matter."

I hadn't much money with me, most of our savings being in Jeanne's handbag. I could have got a job. I wasn't unwilling to work.

For the moment, though, I wanted to keep my status as a refugee. Above all, I wanted to stay in this camp, near the port, near the boats, and to roam among the huts where women were washing their linen and hanging it out to dry, where children were crawling about on the ground, their bottoms bare.

I hadn't left Fumay to have to think and take on responsibilities.

"If I had told them I was a Czech…"

"You are a Czech?"

"From Prague, with Jewish blood from my mother. My mother is Jewish."

She didn't speak in the past tense, which suggested that her mother was still alive.

"I haven't got my passport. I left it behind at Namur. With my accent they might have taken me for a German woman."

I must admit that a disagreeable thought occurred to me and my face clouded over. Wasn't it she who had as it were chosen me, almost immediately after our departure from Fumay?

In our car, I was the only man under fifty, apart from the boy with the blankets. I had nearly forgotten my former schoolmate Leroy, and now I wonder all of a sudden why he wasn't in the army.

In any case I hadn't made any advances. It was she who had come to me. I recalled her precise gestures, the first night, next to Julie and her horse dealer.

She hadn't any luggage, any money; she had ended up by begging a cigarette.

"What are you thinking about?"

"You."

"I know. But what are you thinking?"

I was thinking that she had foreseen, as far back as Fumay, that sooner or later she would be asked for her papers, and that she had provided herself in advance with a guarantor. Me!

We were standing between two huts. There was still a little trampled grass left on the path; some washing was drying on clotheslines. I saw her pupils narrow, her eyes mist over. I wouldn't have thought her capable of crying, and yet they were real tears which were trickling down her cheeks.

At the same time her fists clenched and her face grew so dark that I thought that she was going to hurl a torrent of reproaches and abuse at me through her tears.

I tried to take her hand, which she snatched away.

"Forgive me, Anna."

She shook her head, scattering her hair over her cheeks.

"I didn't really think that. It was just a vague idea, the sort we all have at certain moments."

"I know."

"You understand me?"

She wiped her eyes with the back of her hand, sniveling unaffectedly.

"It's finished," she announced.

"Did I hurt you badly?"

"I'll get over it."

"I hurt myself too. Stupidly. I realized right away that it wasn't true."

"You're sure of that?"

"Yes."

"Come along."

She took me off toward the quayside and we both looked across the masts rocked by the tide at the two bulky towers, like fortress keeps, which flanked the entrance of the port.

"Anna!"

I spoke in an undertone, without turning to look at her, my eyes dazzled by the sunlight and colors.

"Yes?"

"I love you."

"Hush!"

Her throat swelled as if she were swallowing her saliva. Then she spoke of something else, in a voice which had become natural again.

"You aren't afraid of somebody pinching your things?"

I started laughing, laughing as if I would never stop, and I kissed her while seagulls, in their flight, passed a few feet above us.

6

THERE ARE THE OFFICIAL LANDMARKS, THE
dates, which must be available in books. I suppose that everybody, depending on the place where he was at that time,
his family responsibilities, his personal anxieties, has his
own landmarks. Mine are all connected with the reception
center, the center as we used to call it, and distinguished by
the arrival of a certain train, by the fitting out of a new hut,
by an apparently commonplace incident.

Without knowing it, we had been among the first to arrive, a couple of days after the trains had unloaded some
Belgian refugees, so that the center hadn't been broken in
yet.

Had the huts, which had been put up a few weeks before and were still new, been intended for this purpose? The
question never occurred to me. Probably the answer is yes,
seeing that, long before the German attack, the authorities
had evacuated part of Alsace.

Nobody, in any case, expected things to happen so
quickly, and it was obvious that the people in charge of the
camp were improvising from day to day.

On the morning we arrived, the newspapers were already talking of fighting at Monthermé and on the Semois;
the next day the Germans were building bridges for their

tanks at Dinant; and on May 15th, unless I am mistaken, at the same time as the withdrawal of the French government was announced, the daily papers quoted in large type the names of places in our part of the world, Montmédy, Raucourt, Rethel, which we had had so much trouble reaching.

All this admittedly existed for me as it did for the others, but it was happening in a far-off, theoretical world from which I was, as it were, detached.

I should like to try to define my state of mind, not only in the early days, but during the whole time I spent at the center.

The war existed, more tangible with every day that passed, and very real, as we had discovered for ourselves when our train had been machine-gunned. Dazed and bewildered, we had crossed a chaotic zone where there had been no fighting as yet but where battles would follow one after another.

Now that had happened. The names of towns and villages, which we had read in passing, in the sunshine, could now be read in big letters on the front page of the newspapers.

That zone, beyond which we had been surprised to find people coming out of church and towns in their Sunday best, was extending every day, and other trains were following the same route as ours, other cars were shuddering along the roads, bumper to bumper, with mattresses and prams on top, old men and dolls inside.

This long caterpillar had already reached La Rochelle, crawling past us in the direction of Bordeaux.

Men, women, and children were dying as our engineer had died, their eyes staring up into the blue sky. Others were bleeding like the old man who had held his reddened handkerchief to his face, or groaning like the woman with her shoulder shot away.

I ought to be ashamed of admitting it: I didn't participate in this drama. It was outside us. It no longer affected us personally.

It was as if I had known, when I had left Fumay, what I was going to find: a little circle made to measure for me, which would become my shelter and in which it was essential for me to establish myself.

Since the reception center was intended for Belgian refugees, we had no right to be there, Anna and I. That is why we made ourselves as inconspicuous as possible, forgoing the first distributions of soup for fear of being noticed.

A low kitchen range had been installed in the open air, then two, then three, then four, with huge copper pans, real vats, like those used on farms for cooking pig-food.

Later a new prefabricated hut was put up to serve as a kitchen, with fixed tables at which we could sit down to eat.

Followed by Anna, who never left me, I watched the comings and goings. I had soon understood the organization of the camp, which was in fact a continuous improvisation.

One man was in charge of the whole camp, a Belgian, the man who had questioned me on my arrival and whom I avoided as much as possible. He was helped by a number of girls and scouts, including some older scouts from Ostend who had come off one of the first trains.

The refugees were sorted out as well as possible into the useful and useless, that is to say those who were capable of working and those—old men, women, and children—who could only be given shelter.

Theoretically the camp was a stop where people shouldn't have spent more than a few hours or a night.

The factories engaged on defense work, at Aytré, La Pallice, and elsewhere, were clamoring for labor, and wood-cutters were needed in a nearby forest to keep the bakeries supplied with firewood.

Coaches took the skilled workers and their families to these places, where local committees tried to find accommodations for them.

As for the unaccompanied women, the fatherless families, the unemployable persons, they were sent to towns which hadn't any industry, such as Saintes or Royan.

The aim we set ourselves, Anna and I, right away, was to stay at the camp and get ourselves accepted there.

The nurse who had come in a car to bring us food on the last evening of our journey was called Madame Bauche and struck me as the most important person, so that, like a schoolboy who wants to get into his teacher's good books, I gave her all my attention.

She was not very tall, plump, almost fat, aged, as I have said already, between thirty and forty, and I have never seen anybody display so much energy with such unruffled good humor.

I don't know whether she was a registered nurse. She belonged to the upper crust of La Rochelle society, and was married to a doctor or an architect, I can't remember which, for there were four or five other women with her, from the same place, and I used to get their husbands' jobs mixed up.

As soon as a train was announced, she was the first at the station, not, like a lot of others, wearing arm bands, to distribute kind words and chocolate, but to find out those in the crowd who were most in need of help.

As the invasion gathered speed, they became more and more numerous, and she could be seen taking the cripples, the babies, the more helpless of the old people into one of the huts, where, on her knees, in a white smock, she washed sore feet, dressed wounds, and led behind a blanket, which did duty as a curtain, those women who needed special attention.

More often than not she was still there at midnight, making a silent tour of inspection with the aid of a pocket flashlight, comforting women in tears, scolding men who were making too much noise.

The electric system, which had been installed in a hurry, was unsatisfactory, and when I offered to repair it Madame Bauche asked me:

"Do you know about that sort of thing?"

"It's my trade, in a manner of speaking. All I need is a ladder."

"Go and find one."

I had noticed a building under construction in a group of new blocks of flats. I went to the site, and as there was nobody there to ask, I walked off with a ladder with Anna helping me. That ladder stayed at the camp as long as I did, without anybody coming to claim it.

I also replaced some broken windows, mended some taps and water pipes. Madame Bauche didn't know my surname, or where I came from. She called me Marcel and got into the habit of sending for me whenever anything went wrong.

After two or three days I had become the general handyman. Leroy had disappeared with the first batch, sent off in the direction of Bordeaux or Toulouse. Of all the people in our car, old Jules was the only one who remained at the camp, where he was tolerated because he played the fool.

In town I met the man with the pipe, the one I used to call the concierge. Looking very harassed, he told me in passing that he was on his way to the Prefecture to demand news of his wife, and I never saw him again.

That happened on the second or third day. The day before, Anna had washed her panties and her brassiere, which she had hung out to dry in the sun, and as we wandered about the camp we exchanged conspiratorial glances at the thought that she was naked under her black dress.

There was a big tower at the end of the quay, the Clock Tower, which was a more massive construction than those flanking the entrance to the port, and which you went under to get to the main street.

This archway was to become a familiar sight for us, as were the arcaded streets which were unbelievably busy, for, over and above the population and the refugees, the town had troops and sailors stationed in it.

When I suggested buying Anna a change of underwear, she made no objection. It was essential. I had wondered whether I might not take the opportunity to buy her a light-colored dress of the sort you could see in all the shop windows. She must have thought about it too, for she guessed everything that entered my head.

"You know," I said to her, "I'd offer to give you a dress…" She didn't feel obliged to protest politely, as so many others would have done, if only as a matter of form, and she looked at me with a smile.

"Well? What were you going to add?"

"That I hesitate to do so, out of selfishness. For me, your black dress is almost part of you. You understand? I wonder whether I wouldn't be disappointed to see you wearing something else."

"I'm happy as I am," she murmured, squeezing my fingertips.

I could feel that that was true. I was happy too. As we were passing a cosmetics shop I stopped.

"You don't use powder or lipstick?"

"I used to, before."

She didn't mean before me, but before Namur.

"Would you like to have some again?"

"That depends on you. Only if you prefer me with makeup."

"No."

"Then I'd rather not."

She didn't want to have her hair cut either; it was neither long nor short.

There was something I never thought about, not only because I refused to think about it, but because it never entered my head: the fact that our life together didn't have any future.

I didn't know what was going to happen. Nobody could know. We were living through an interval, outside space, and I savored those days and nights greedily.

I was greedy for everything, for the changing spectacle of the port and the sea, the fishing boats of different colors which went off in Indian file at high tide, the fish which was unloaded in baskets or flat boxes, the crowds in the streets, glimpses of the camp and the station.

I was even hungrier for Anna, and for the first time in my life I wasn't ashamed of my sexual desires.

On the contrary. With her, it had become a game which struck me as very pure. We talked about it gaily, frankly, inventing a whole code, adopting a certain number of signs which allowed us to exchange certain secret thoughts in public.

The center of this new world was the greenish tent which could be seen from a long way off dominating the huts, and, inside this tent, our own corner in the straw, what we called our stable.

We had arranged our belongings there, the things I had taken out of my luggage and other things which I had bought, such as mess tins for the soup and a compact spirit stove with everything we needed to brew our morning coffee, outside, between a couple of huts, facing the boats.

The others, especially those who were only staying there for a night, looked at our corner in surprise and, I feel sure, with envy, just as I in the past had sometimes looked at a real stable, with horses living snugly on their litter.

I used to talk about our litter too, and I didn't like changing our straw too often, so that it remained impregnated with us.

It wasn't only there that we made love, but all over the place, often in the most unexpected spots. That had begun with the boat one evening when we were looking at the fishing smacks rocking beside the quay while the creaking of the pulleys imitated the cry of the seagulls.

Knowing that in all probability I would never go to sea, I looked longingly at the open hatchway of one of the boats, whose deck was piled with lobster pots. Next my eyes turned to Anna, then back to the boat, and she started laughing with a laugh which formed part of our secret language.

"You want to?"

"What about you?"

"You aren't afraid we might be taken for thieves and arrested?"

It was after midnight. The quay was deserted, all the lights camouflaged. Any footsteps could be heard a long way off. The hardest thing about it was going down the iron ladder embedded in the stone. The last few rungs were slimy.

We managed all the same and slipped through the hatchway into the darkness below, where we bumped into more baskets, cans, and objects we couldn't identify.

There was a smell of fish, seaweed, and paraffin. Finally Anna said:

"This way..."

I found her hand, which guided me along, and the two of us collapsed onto a hard, narrow bunk, pushing aside some oilskins which were in our way.

The tide rocked us gently to and fro. Through the hatchway we could see a patch of sky and a few stars; a train whistled over by the station. It wasn't a new arrival. Some carriages were moving backward and forward, shunting around as if they were trying to tidy up the tracks.

There were no fences yet around the camp. We could come in and go out as we liked. There was nobody mounting guard. We just had to move softly so as not to wake our neighbors.

Later on, fences were put up, not to shut us in, but to prevent prowlers from mixing with the refugees and stealing things, as had happened once or twice.

Often, too, in the evening, we used to roam around the station, and one night when there was no traffic we lay down on the bench farthest away from the station buildings.

That amused us. It was a sort of challenge, and once we made love behind some bales of straw, close to Madame Bauche, who was bandaging sore feet and talking to us at the same time.

Every day I devoted a certain amount of time to looking

for my wife and daughter to the best of my ability.

They hadn't been deceiving us, I can't remember where, at Auxerre or Saumur, or perhaps it was at Tours, when they had told us of lists which would be posted up. Some were beginning to appear on the door of the office, where groups collected every morning to consult them.

Only they were lists of Belgian refugees. A lot of them were at Bordeaux, at Saintes, at Cognac, at Angoulême. Some had gone as far as Toulouse, and a good many were living in villages I had never heard of before.

I looked through the lists just in case. Every day, too, I went to see an official at the station who had promised to find out what had become of our train. He had made it a point of honor and it annoyed him intensely to be unable to find any trace of it.

"A train can't disappear like that," he muttered, "even in wartime. Sooner or later, I'm bound to find out where it's gone."

Thanks to the block telephone system linking one station to another, he had put his colleagues on the trail, and they were beginning to talk about the ghost train.

We went to the town hall, Anna and I. Crowds used to gather outside all the offices, for at that time everybody needed a piece of information, a permit, a paper bearing an official stamp.

Here too lists were posted up, of French people this time, but my wife's name still wasn't on them.

"If you're looking for somebody, you'd do better to try the Prefecture."

We went there. The courtyard was bright, the corridors and the offices bathed in sunshine, with clerks in shirt sleeves and a lot of girls in summer dresses. I had left Anna in the street, seeing that I couldn't pass her off as my wife when it was my wife I was trying to trace.

I saw her from the window, standing on the curb, raising her head, then walking up and down, grave, thoughtful. Already I felt impatient to rejoin her, and I reproached myself for leaving her, even for such a short time.

They were issuing petrol coupons to motorists. The Place d'Armes, the quays, the streets were crowded with hundreds of cars from all points of the compass. Their owners were here, at the Prefecture, waiting in the longest of the queues for the precious coupon which would enable them to continue their exodus.

The day before, in the line of cars making their way toward Rochefort, I had caught sight of a hearse from Charleroi in which a whole family was installed, and I suppose that their luggage was occupying the place of the coffin.

"Are you looking for something?"

"I'd like to know where my wife…"

It seems that there were already thousands of us, and there would soon be tens of thousands, in the same plight. Not only were people still fleeing from Belgium and the north, but panic had taken hold of the Parisians since the government had left the city, and it was said that, apart from the cars, a long procession of men and women on foot was now winding along the roads.

In the villages close to the main roads, the bakers' shops were being taken by storm, and there wasn't a single bed available in the hospitals.

"Fill out this form. Leave me your name and address."

Out of prudence, I didn't mention the reception center and I put down *poste restante*. Already, however, old Jules and I were no longer the only French people in the camp.

I can still picture to myself the ugliest train, in the heat of a fine afternoon, when the girls of a local school had just gone by, in a line, along the pavement, on their way to a fête.

What we, like Madame Bauche, called ugly trains were those which had suffered the most en route, trains in which people had died, in which women had given birth without proper attention.

There had been a lunatics' train, for instance, ten carriages full of lunatics evacuated from an asylum. In spite of all the precautions taken, two of them escaped and got as far as the big clock before they were caught.

I can't remember whether the train I am talking about had come from Douai or from Laon, for I tend to get the two towns mixed up. It was carrying only a few wounded people, who had had medical attention on the way, but the eyes of all the passengers, men, women, and children, were still glazed with terror.

One woman was trembling violently and she went on trembling all night, her teeth chattering and her hands pushing away her blanket.

Others talked incoherently or kept on repeating the same story in a monotonous voice.

They were being entrained, at Douai or at Laon, two hundred yards from the station which was packed with people. Some of them were waiting for late-comers or for relatives who had gone to the refreshment room to buy something when, without any warning having been sounded, some planes had suddenly appeared in the sky.

"The bombs fell like that, Monsieur... Sideways... You could see them falling on the station and the houses opposite, and everything started trembling and blowing up, roofs, stones, people, the carriages standing a little way off... I saw a leg hurled into the air, and I myself, although we were a fair distance away, I was thrown to the ground on top of my son..."

The sirens had finally started wailing, those of the fire engines too, and from the heaps of stones, bricks, and twisted metal corpses could be seen poking out, pieces of broken furniture, occasionally a familiar object which had miraculously remained intact.

The newspapers announced the formation of a new government, the retreat toward Dunkirk, the blocking of railway lines all over the place, while Anna and I continued our quiet existence as if it were going to last forever.

Anna knew as well as I did that this wasn't so, but she never made any mention of it. Before me, she had shared other existences, other more or less prolonged moments of different lives, and I preferred not to think about what was going to happen after me.

It had wrung my heart seeing her from the window in the Prefecture, alone on the pavement, as if we were already parted. I had been filled with panic. When I had rejoined her, I had seized hold of her arm as if I had been separated from her for several days.

I would be ready to swear that it didn't rain once during the whole of that period apart from a solitary storm, I remember that now, which left pockets of water in the roof of our tent. The weather seemed unreal, it was so wonderful, and I can't imagine La Rochelle otherwise than in the heat of the sun.

The fishermen used to bring us fish. The scouts, every morning, went around the market, where their baskets were filled with vegetables and fruit. They had a handcart like the one which I had abandoned at Fumay in the station yard. I accompanied them several times, putting myself between the shafts for the fun of it, while Anna followed on the pavement.

We nearly had some ugly incidents, in the camp and at the station, when the radio announced the capitulation of Belgium. At that time there were almost as many French refugees as Belgians, and whole factories were being evacuated. I saw some Flemings and Walloons who were crying like children, and others who came to blows and had to be separated.

Every day that passed nibbled away some of my meager capital of happiness. That isn't the right word, but as I can't find another, and as people are always talking about happiness, I am obliged to make do with the word myself.

Sooner or later, at the town hall, at the Prefecture, at the post office, I would find news of Jeanne and my daughter. The baby was nearly due, and I hoped that the journey and all the excitement hadn't brought on a premature delivery.

The Paris newspapers were publishing lists of readers who gave news to their families in that way, and for a moment I thought of using the same method. But at Fumay we never read any of the Paris papers. Which was I to choose? We would have had to agree on one beforehand, something which we hadn't done. There was no likelihood of Jeanne buying all the daily papers every day.

The Germans were advancing so fast that there was a lot of talk of treason and fifth-column activities. It appeared that in one of our huts they had arrested a man who said he was Dutch, and who had a portable radio transmitter in his luggage.

I don't know whether that was true. Madame Bauche, whom I asked about it, couldn't confirm the story, but she had seen some plain-clothes detectives prowling around the camp.

This frightened Anna, whose surname, Kupfer, sounded very Teutonic. We thought about that every time we crossed the square between the camp and the station and looked at the geraniums in all their splendor.

The municipal gardener had set them out, already in flower, shortly after our arrival. I remember seeing him, early in the morning, in the as yet pale sunshine, doing his reassuring work, when the refugee trains were arriving all the time at the station and the newspapers on the stall were full of disasters.

It seems that two hours later, while the gardener was still there, a German radio station, which broadcast propaganda in French, said something to this effect:

"It is kind of you, Monsieur Vieiljeux, to plant flowers outside your station in our honor. We shall be there a few days from now."

Monsieur Vieiljeux, whom I never saw, was the Mayor of La Rochelle, and the German radio went on sending him ironic messages, thus showing that they knew everything that was happening in the town.

The word "spy" could be heard more and more often, and people's eyes became suspicious.

"You'd better speak as little as possible when other people are around."

"I've thought of that."

She wasn't talkative. Nor was I. Even if both of us had been, there were so many forbidden subjects between us that we wouldn't have found much to say to each other.

No past or future. Nothing but a fragile present, which we sipped and savored together.

We feasted ourselves on little pleasures, on patterns of light and shade which we knew we should remember all our lives. As for our flesh, we tortured it with our desperate efforts to blend it into a single whole.

I am not ashamed to say that I was happy, with a happiness which bore the same relation to everyday happiness as the sound produced by passing a violin bow across the wrong side of the bridge bears to the normal sound of a violin. It was sharp and exquisite, and deliciously painful.

As for our sexual hunger, I am almost certain that we weren't alone in feeling it. Although we were not as crowded in the circus tent as in our cattle car, there were still about a hundred of us, men and women, sleeping under the same shelter. Not a night went by without my hearing bodies moving cautiously, panting breath and amorous complaints.

I wasn't alone in feeling outside ordinary life and its conventions. At any moment planes might appear in the sky and drop their rosary of bombs. In a fortnight or three weeks the German troops would be at La Rochelle, and nobody had any idea what would happen then.

The first time the air-raid warning sounded, we were told to lie down beside the dock, for the underground shelter which had been built near the freight station was too far away.

The anti-aircraft guns opened up. Bursts of fire came from the station. Later we were told that it was a mistake, that the planes had been French machines which hadn't given the regulation signals.

Some other planes dived over the town to lay mines around a ship, the *Champlain*, in the La Pallice roadstead. In the morning the boat blew up. We heard the explosions without knowing what was happening.

Later on, some petrol tanks started blazing two or three miles from the town, and black smoke hung in the sky for several days.

I have said this before, but I say it again: the days went by both fast and slowly. The notion of time had altered. The Germans were entering Paris, whereas Anna and I had changed nothing in our little habits. Only the atmosphere in the station was altering from day to day, becoming more confused and chaotic.

As at Fumay, I got up first and went outside to make the coffee, at the same time shaving in front of a mirror hooked onto the canvas of the tent. Part of one hut had finally been set aside as a washroom for the women, and Anna went there early, before the rush.

Then we used to stroll over to the station, where they were used to us and gave us a cheery greeting.

"Many trains today?"

"We're expecting some personnel from Renault's."

We knew the subway, the tracks, the benches. It was with a certain tenderness that we looked at the cattle cars in which there was still some straw lying about. Where was ours now, in which a little of our own smell must be lingering?

After that, Madame Bauche nearly always needed me for some job, mending a door or a window, or fitting up new shelves for food or medical supplies.

We went for our ration of soup. Now and then we gave ourselves an extra treat. Crossing the avenue, we would go into a cozy bar where I knew Anna liked to drink an apéritif while I, to keep her company, ordered a lemonade.

In the afternoon we went into town, and I would go and read the lists before dropping in at the post office.

Unless it was a little premature, our child might be born any day now, and I kept wondering who would look after Sophie while my wife was in the maternity home.

Oddly enough, I couldn't manage to picture either of them in my mind. Their features remained vague and blurred.

I wasn't too worried about Sophie, for we had had a couple of children in the camp for a week who had lost their mother on the way and didn't suffer as a result. They played with the others, as carefree as they were, and when their mother finally came to fetch them they stood motionless in front of her for quite a while, embarrassed, as if they had been playing truant.

The 16th of June is one of the dates I remember. Pétain, at Orléans, was asking for an armistice and some soldiers left the station suddenly, without their weapons, in spite of attempts by the officers to stop them.

Three days later the Germans were at Nantes. We calculated that, being motorized, they were moving fast, and we expected to see them the following day.

But it wasn't until the 22nd, a Saturday, that some motorists called out to us in passing:

"They're at La Roche-sur-Yon!"

"Have you seen them?"

They nodded as they drove on.

The following night was hot. Anna lay down first, and, standing there, I felt tears coming to my eyes at the sight of her making her hole in the straw. I said:

"No. Come along."

She never asked me where or why. You would have sworn that she had spent her life following a man, that she had been born to do just that.

We walked along listening to the sound of the sea and the creaking of the rigging. Perhaps she thought that I was looking for the shelter of a boat?

I led her like that as far as the end of the port, where the building yards begin, and then I turned into the path which ends up at the beach.

There wasn't a sound to be heard. You couldn't see any lights in the town, nothing but a dark green lantern at the end of the jetty.

We lay down on the sand, near the little waves, and we stayed for a long time without saying anything, without doing anything, listening to our heartbeats.

"Anna! I'd like you to remember always…"

"Hush!"

She didn't need words. She didn't like them. I think they frightened her.

I started to take her, awkwardly, gradually bringing to my lovemaking an impatience which resembled malice. This time she didn't help me, but lay motionless, her eyes fixed on my face, and I could read no expression in them.

For a moment it seemed to me that she had already gone and I imagined her alone again, like a lost animal.

"Anna!" I cried, in the same voice in which I would have called for help. "Try to understand!"

She took my head between her hands to murmur, choking back her sobs:

"It was good!"

She wasn't speaking of our embrace but of us, of all that had been us for such a short time. We wept, one on top of the other, while we made love. Meanwhile the sea had come up to our feet.

I needed to do something, I didn't know what. I tore her dress off her, stripped off my clothes. I said once again:

"Come along!"

The sky was bright enough for her body to stand out in the dark, but I couldn't see her face. Was she really frightened? Did she think that I meant to drown her, perhaps drown myself with her? Her body drew back, seized by an animal panic.

"Come along, silly!"

I ran into the water, where she soon joined me. She could swim. I couldn't. She went farther into the sea, then came and made rings around me.

I wonder today whether she was so very far wrong to feel frightened. Everything was possible just then. We tried to make a game of that bath, to amuse ourselves like schoolchildren on holiday, but we didn't succeed.

"Are you cold?"

"No."

"Let's run to get warm."

We ran along the sand, which stuck to our feet and the calves of our legs.

It hadn't been a good idea. On our way back to the camp, a patrol obliged us to stay hidden in a corner for nearly a quarter of an hour.

Our tent seemed to stifle us with human warmth, and after we finally curled up in our corner I didn't sleep all night.

The next day was a Sunday. Some of the refugees dressed up to go to mass. In town we saw girls in light-colored dresses, children in their Sunday best walking in front of their parents. The confectioners' shops were open and I bought a cake which was still warm, as at Fumay.

After lunch we went to eat it beside the dock, sitting on the stone with our legs dangling above the water.

At five o'clock some German motorcyclists stopped outside the town hall and an officer asked to see Monsieur Vieiljeux.

7

ON MONDAY MORNING I FELT EMPTY AND depressed. Anna had had a restless night, shaken several times by those abrupt movements which I found it hard to get used to, and several times she had spoken volubly in her native language.

I got up at the same time as on the other days to make the coffee and to shave, but, instead of finding myself alone outside, I saw some groups of half-awake refugees who were watching German motorcyclists going past.

I had the impression of finding in their eyes the mournful resignation which they must have been able to read in mine, and that was a general reaction: it lasted several days, for some people several weeks.

A page had been turned. An epoch had ended, everybody felt sure of that, although nobody could foresee what was going to take its place.

It was no longer just our fate which was at stake but that of the world to which we belonged.

We had formed a more or less terrifying idea of the war, of the invasion, and now, just as war and invasion reached us in our turn, we saw that they were different from everything we had imagined. It is true that this was just the beginning.

For example, while my water was boiling on the little spirit stove on the ground and the Germans were still going by without bothering about us, very young, pink, and fresh as if they were going on parade, I could see two French soldiers, with their rifles slung over their shoulders, mounting guard at the door of the station.

No trains had arrived for two days. The platforms were deserted, as were the waiting rooms, the refreshment room, and the military commandant's office. The two soldiers, not having received any orders, didn't know what to do, and it wasn't until about nine o'clock that they propped their rifles against the wall and went off.

While I was lathering my cheeks with my shaving brush I heard the familiar sound of diesel engines and some boats went out fishing. There were only three or four of them. The fact remains that, while the enemy was invading the town, some fishermen went out to sea as usual to cast their nets. Nobody stopped them.

When we went toward the town, Anna and I, the cafés, the bars, the shops were open, and shopkeepers were tidying up their window displays. I remember in particular a florist arranging carnations in some buckets in front of her shop. Did that mean there were people buying flowers on a day like that?

On the pavements people were walking along, rather worried, above all perplexed, as I was, and there were some men in uniform, Frenchmen, among the crowd.

One of them, in the middle of the Rue du Palais, was asking a policeman what he ought to do, and, judging by his gestures, I gathered that the policeman was replying that he didn't know any more than the soldier did.

I didn't see any Germans in the vicinity of the town

hall. To tell the truth, I don't remember seeing any walking among the townspeople. I went to consult the lists, as on other days, then on to the post office, where I waited my turn at the *poste restante* counter while Anna stood pensively by the window.

We had said scarcely anything to each other since the morning. We were both of us equally depressed, and when I was handed a message in my name I wasn't surprised, I thought that it was inevitable, that it was bound to happen that particular day.

But I went weak at the knees and had some difficulty in walking away from the counter.

I knew already. The form was printed on poor paper, with blanks which had been completed in purple pencil.

NAME OF MISSING PERSON: Jeanne Marie Clémentine Féron, *née* Van Straeten.

PLACE OF ORIGIN: Fumay (Ardennes).

PROFESSION: None.

MISSING SINCE: _____

METHOD OF TRANSPORT: Rail.

ACCOMPANIED BY: Her daughter, aged four.

PRESENT WHEREABOUTS: _____

My heart started beating wildly and I looked around for Anna.

I saw her against the light, still by the window, gazing at me without moving.

PRESENT WHEREABOUTS: Maternity home at Bressuire.

I went over to her and held out the paper without a word. Then, without really knowing what I was doing, I made for the telephone counter.

"Is it possible to telephone to Bressuire?"

I expected to be told that it wasn't. Contrary to all logic, it seemed to me, the telephone was working normally.

"What number do you want?"

"The maternity home."

"Don't you know the number? Or the name of the street?"

"I imagine there's only one maternity home in the town."

In my memories of geography lessons at school, Bressuire was somewhere in a region you rarely heard about, between Niort and Poitiers, farther west, toward the Vendée.

"There's a delay of ten minutes."

Anna had given me back the message, which I stuffed into my pocket. I said, unnecessarily, since she knew it already:

"I'm waiting for them to put the call through."

She lit a cigarette. I had bought her a cheap handbag as well as a little suitcase in imitation leather in which to keep her underwear and her toilet things. The floor of the post office was still marked by the drops of water which had been sprinkled on it before it was swept.

Opposite, on the other side of a little square, some men who looked like local notabilities were sitting on a café terrace, arguing and drinking white wine, and the proprietor of the café, in shirt sleeves and a blue apron, was standing near them, holding a napkin.

"Bressuire is on the line in Box 2."

At the other end of the line a voice was getting impatient.

"Hello! La Rochelle… Speak up."

"Is that Bressuire?"

"Yes, of course it is. I'm putting you through."

"Hello. Is that the maternity home?"

"Who's speaking?"

"Marcel Féron, I'd like to know if my wife is still there."

"What name did you say?"

"Féron."

I had to spell it out: F for Fernand, and so on.

"Has she had a baby here?"

"I suppose so. She was pregnant when…"

"Is she in a private room or a public ward?"

"I don't know. We are refugees from Fumay and I lost her on the way as well as my daughter."

"Hold the line. I'll go and see."

Through the glass pane of the phone booth I saw Anna, who was leaning on the windowsill, and it had a curious effect on me, looking at her black dress, her shoulders, her lips which were becoming unfamiliar to me again.

"Yes, she's here. She gave birth the day before yesterday."

"Can I speak to her?"

"There's no telephone in the wards, but I can give her a message."

"Tell her… "

I started searching for something to say and suddenly I heard a crackling sound on the line.

"Hello!… Hello!… Don't cut me off, Mademoiselle…"

"Speak up, then… Hurry up."

"Tell her that her husband is at La Rochelle, that all's well, that he'll come to Bressuire as quickly as he can.… I don't know yet if I can find any transport but…"

There was nobody on the line anymore and I didn't know if she had heard the end of my sentence. It hadn't occurred to me to ask whether it was a boy or a girl, or whether everything had gone well.

I went to pay at the counter. Then I said automatically, as I had said so often in the course of the last few weeks:

"Come along."

It was unnecessary, seeing that Anna always followed me. In the street she asked:

"How are you going to get there?"

"I don't know."

"They probably won't get the trains running again for several days."

I didn't ask myself any questions. I would go to Bressuire on foot if necessary. Seeing that I knew where Jeanne was, I had to join her. It wasn't a matter of duty. It was so natural that I didn't hesitate for a moment.

I must have appeared very calm and sure of myself, for Anna was looking at me with a certain astonishment. On the quay I stopped at the shop where I had bought the spirit stove. It had some coarse canvas kit bags for sale and I wanted one to replace the trunk which, even empty, was too heavy to be carted along the roads.

The German soldiers were still not mixing with the passersby. A group which had camped on the outskirts of the town, on the old ramparts, around a field kitchen, had gone off again at dawn.

I went for the last time into the camp, into the green circus tent, where I stuffed the contents of the trunk into the kit bag. Noticing the spirit stove, I handed it to Anna.

"You can have this. I won't need it anymore, and in any case I haven't got room for it."

She took it without protest and put it in her suitcase. I was preoccupied, wondering where and how we were going to say goodbye.

Some women were still asleep, and others, who were busy with their children, looked at us inquisitively.

"I'll help you."

Anna hoisted the kit bag onto my shoulder and I bent down to pick up the suitcase. She followed me, holding her case. Outside, between a couple of huts, I started clumsily:

"All my life…"

She gave me a smile which baffled me.

"I'm coming with you."

"To Bressuire?"

I was worried.

"I want to stay with you as long as possible. Don't worry. When we get there I'll disappear."

I was relieved to see our leave-taking postponed. We didn't meet Madame Bauche and we left, like so many others, without saying goodbye to her and thanking her. Yet we were the oldest inhabitants of the center, for old Jules had been taken to hospital with an attack of delirium tremens.

We made our way toward the Place d'Armes through increasingly chaotic streets. The terrace of the Café de la Paix was crowded. Civilian cars were driving about, and at the far end of the square, near the park, you could make out the mottled camouflage of the German cars.

I didn't expect to find a bus. Yet there were several outside the bus station, since nobody had given orders to suspend the service. I asked if there was a bus for Bressuire or for Niort. They told me no, that the road to Niort was jammed with cars and with refugees on foot, and that the Germans were finding it difficult to get through.

"There's a bus for Fontenay-le-Comte."

"Is that on the road to Bressuire?"

"It gets you a bit nearer."

"When does it leave?"

"The driver's filling up with petrol."

We installed ourselves in the bus, in the blazing sun-shine, and to begin with we were alone among the empty seats. Then a French soldier got in, a man of about forty, from the country, with his jacket over his arm, and later half a dozen people sat down around us.

Sitting side by side, and shaken by the jolting of the bus, Anna and I kept our eyes fixed on the scenery.

"Are you hungry?"

"No. What about you?"

"I'm not hungry either."

A peasant woman sitting facing us, her eyes red with crying, was eating a slice of pâté which smelled good.

We were following a road which went from village to village, not far from the sea at first, through Nieul, Marsilly, Esnandres, and Charron, and we didn't see many Germans, just a small group in the square of each little town, in front of the church or the town hall, with the local inhabitants watching them from a distance.

We were off the route taken by the refugees and most of the troops. Somewhere, I thought I recognized the meadow and the stop where we had slept on the last night of our journey. I am not sure, because no landscape looks the same from the railway as it does from the road.

We passed a big dairy where dozens of pails of milk were shining in the sun; then we crossed a bridge over a canal, near an inn with an arbor beside it. There were blue checked tablecloths, flowers on the tables, and a fretwork chef at the roadside, holding out a stenciled menu.

At Fontenay-le-Comte there were more Germans, and more vehicles too, including trucks, but only in the main street leading to the station. At the bus station, in a square, we were told that there was no coach for Bressuire.

The idea of hiring a taxi didn't occur to me, first because that was something I had never done, and then because I wouldn't have believed that it was still possible.

We went into a café in the marketplace to have a snack.

"Are you refugees?"

"Yes. From the Ardennes."

"There are some people from the Ardennes working as woodcutters in the Mervent forest. They look a bit wild, but they're good sorts, with plenty of guts. Are you going far?"

"To Bressuire."

"Have you got a car?"

We were the only customers in the place, and an old man in felt slippers came to look at us through the kitchen door.

"No. We'll walk there if need be."

"You think you can walk all the way to Bressuire? With this little lady? Wait a minute while I ask if Martin's truck has gone."

We were lucky. Martin's business, on the other side of the trees, was a wholesale ironmonger's. It had some deliveries to make at Pouzauges and Cholet. We waited, drinking coffee, and looking out at the empty square.

There was room for both of us, squeezed together in the cab, beside the driver, and after a fairly steep hill we drove through an endless forest.

"The Ardennes people are over there," said our driver, pointing to a clearing and a few huts around which some half-naked children were playing.

"Are there many Germans around here?"

"There was a lot of traffic yesterday evening and last night. It will probably start again. What we've seen has been mainly motorbikes and field kitchens. I suppose the tanks are following."

He stopped to leave a parcel at a smithy where a plow-horse turned toward us, neighing. The day seemed terribly long to me, and in spite of our stroke of luck the journey went on and on.

I felt rather annoyed with Anna now for having come with me. It would have been better for both of us to have done with it at La Rochelle, with my kit bag on my shoulder and my suitcase in my hand.

Knowing that I was annoyed, she made herself as inconspicuous as she could between the driver and me. It suddenly occurred to me that her warm hip was touching the driver's, and I felt a surge of jealousy.

We took nearly two hours to get to Pouzauges, meeting nobody but a motorized column half a mile long. The soldiers looked at us as they went by, looked at Anna above all, and a few of them waved to her.

"You're only about fifteen miles from Bressuire. You'd better come into this café with me. I might be able to get you a lift."

Some surly-looking men were playing cards. Two others, at the back of the room, were arguing over some papers spread out between the glasses.

"Look, is anybody going Bressuire way? This lady and gentleman are refugees who have to get there before tonight."

One of the men who was arguing and who looked like an estate agent inspected Anna from head to foot before saying:

"I can take them as far as Cerizay."

I didn't know where Cerizay was. They explained that it was halfway to Bressuire. I had expected to have to overcome difficulties and show a certain heroism in order to rejoin my wife, to tramp the roads for several days and to be harassed by the Germans.

I was almost disappointed that everything was going so easily. We waited for an hour until the discussion ended. Several times the men stood up and made as if to shake hands, only to sit down again and order another round of drinks.

Our new driver had an apoplectic complexion. With a self-important manner he made Anna sit beside him while I installed myself on the backseat. I suddenly felt the fatigue of my sleepless night; my eyelids were heavy and my lips burning hot, as if I had a fever. Perhaps I had got sunstroke?

After some time I ceased to be able to make out the conversation going on in front. I was vaguely aware of meadows, woods, and one or two sleepy-looking villages. We crossed a bridge over a river which was practically dry, before finally stopping in a square.

I thanked the driver. So did Anna. We walked two or three hundred yards before noticing, outside a baker's shop, a flour truck on which the name of a miller at Bressuire was painted.

So I didn't have to do any walking. Nor did Anna. We weren't alone together once all day.

Night had fallen. We were standing on a pavement, near the terrace of a café, with my kit bag and my suitcase at my feet. I turned aside to take a few bank notes out of my wallet. Anna understood and didn't protest when I slipped them into her handbag.

The square was empty all around us. I have never had such an impression of emptiness. I stopped a boy who was passing.

"Can you tell me where the maternity home is?"

"Second street on the left, right at the end. You can't miss it."

Guessing that I was going to say goodbye there and then, Anna murmured:

"Let me go as far as the door with you."

She was so humble that I hadn't the heart to refuse. In one square there were some Germans fussing around a dozen big tanks and some officers shouting orders.

The street with the maternity home was on a slope, lined with middle-class houses. At the far end there was a big brick building.

Once again I put down my kit bag and my suitcase. I didn't dare to look at Anna. A woman was leaning out of a window, a child sitting on the doorstep, and only the roof-tops were still lit by the setting sun.

"Well…" I began.

The sound stopped in my throat and I took hold of her hands.

Despite myself I had to look at her one last time and I saw a face which seemed already blurred and indistinct.

"Goodbye!"

"I hope you'll be happy, Marcel."

I pressed her hands. I let go of them. I picked up my kit bag and my suitcase again, almost staggering, and when I had nearly got to the door of the maternity home she ran up behind me to whisper in my ear:

"I've been happy with you."

Through the glass door I caught sight of some nurses in an entrance hall, a trolley, the receptionist talking on the telephone. I went in. I turned around. She was standing there on the pavement.

"Madame Féron, please."

8

IT WASN'T SIMPLY TO STRAIGHTEN OUT MY ideas, nor in the hope of understanding certain things which have always worried me, that I started writing these recollections, unknown to my wife and everybody else, in a notebook which I lock up every time anybody comes into my office.

For now I have an office, a shop with two display windows in the Rue du Château, and I employ more people than the son of my former employer, Monsieur Ponchot, who hasn't kept up with the times and whose shop is still as dark and solemn as when I used to work there.

I have three growing children, two girls and a boy. It is the boy, Jean-François, who was born at Bressuire while Sophie was being looked after by some farmers in a nearby village who had taken my wife in when the train had abandoned them.

Sophie seemed pleased to see me, but not surprised, and when, a month later, we took the train to Fumay with her mother and her little brother, she was very upset.

The birth had been easy. Jean-François is the sturdiest of the three. It is his younger sister who has given us a lot of trouble. It is true that I found Jeanne edgier than ever, getting frightened about nothing at all, and convinced that misfortune was lying in wait for her.

Isabelle, our third child, was born at the most dramatic moment in the war, when we were waiting for the Allied landing. Some people said that the landing would produce the same chaos and disorder as the German invasion. The authorities expected that all the able-bodied men would be sent to Germany, and routes were marked with arrows so that we shouldn't congest the roads needed by the army.

It was also the time of shortages. Food stocks were at their lowest point and I couldn't afford to buy much on the black market.

The fact remains that Jeanne was delivered prematurely, the baby was put in an incubator, and my wife has never really recovered. I mean morally even more than physically. She is still timid and pessimistic, and when, later on, we moved to the Rue du Château, she was convinced for a long time that we were heading for disaster and that we would end up poorer than ever.

I picked up my life where I had left it, as it was my duty and destiny to do, because that was the only possible solution and I had never imagined that it might be otherwise.

I worked hard. When the time came, I sent my children to the best schools.

I don't know what they are going to do in later life. For the moment they are like all the other children of our sort of world and accept the ideas they are taught.

All the same, especially watching my son growing up, listening to the questions he asks, and seeing the glances he darts at me, all the same I wonder.

Perhaps Jean-François will go on behaving as his mother

and his schoolmasters teach him to and as I do more or less sincerely myself.

It is also possible that one day he may rebel against our ideas, our way of life, and try to be himself.

That is true of the girls as well, of course, but it was when I tried to imagine Jean-François as a young man that I started feeling worried.

My hair has receded. I need glasses with increasingly thick lenses. I am a fairly prosperous, quiet, rather dull man. From a certain point of view, the pair we form, Jeanne and I, is really a caricature of the married couple.

And then the idea came to me of leaving my son another picture of myself. I wondered whether it wouldn't do him good, one day, to know that his father hadn't always been the shopkeeper and the timid husband he had known, with no ambition beyond that of bringing up his children to the best of his ability and helping them to climb a small rung of the social ladder.

Like that, my son, and perhaps my daughters too, would learn that there had been a different man in me, and that for a few weeks I had been capable of a real passion.

I don't know yet. I haven't made up my mind what to do with this notebook, and I hope that I have some time left in which to think it over.

In any case, I owed it to myself to reveal that idea of mine here, just as I owe it to myself, in order to be honest with myself and other people, to go on to the end of the story.

As early as the winter of 1940, life had almost gone back to normal, except for the presence of the Germans and the food situation, which was already getting difficult. I had gone back to work. Radio sets were not prohibited, and more of them were being bought than ever before. Nestor, the cock, and our hens, minus one, had returned to the bottom of the garden, and, contrary to my expectations, nothing had been stolen from the house, not a single radio, not a single tool; my workshop was just as I had left it, except for the dust.

The spring and the autumn of 1941 must have been uneventful, for I can remember very little about them except that Dr. Wilhems was a frequent caller. Jeanne's health was worrying him, and he later admitted to me that he was afraid of her having a nervous breakdown.

Although there has never been any mention of Anna between my wife and myself, I would swear that she knows. Did some rumor reach her ears, spread by refugees who had returned home like us? I can't remember meeting any at the time, but it isn't impossible.

In any case, that had nothing to do with her health or her worries. She has never been a passionate or a jealous woman, and, like her sister Berthe, whose husband, the confectioner, is said to be a ladykiller, she wouldn't mind me having affairs, provided they were kept discreet and didn't endanger our home.

I am not trying to get rid of my responsibilities. I am saying what I think, quite objectively. If she realized, at Bressuire, that for a while I had stopped being the same man, my behavior, from then on, reassured her.

Did she guess that she had nearly lost me? But that isn't really true. Our marriage hadn't been in any serious danger: I say that at the risk of diminishing myself in my own eyes.

It was mainly the Germans that frightened her, filling her with an instinctive, physical fear: their footsteps in the street, their music, the posters which they put up on the walls and which always announced bad news.

On account of my trade, they had ransacked my workshop and the house twice, and had even dug holes in the garden in search of secret radio transmitters.

We were still living in the same street at that time, near the quay, between the old Matrays' house and that of the schoolmaster with the curly-haired daughter. The schoolmaster and his family hadn't returned and we didn't see them again until after the Liberation, for they spent the whole of the war near Carcassonne, where he was in the Resistance.

As far as I can remember, the winter of 1941–42 was a very cold one. Shortly before Christmas, when there had already been some snow, Dr. Wilhems called one morning to see Jeanne, who was just recovering from an attack of influenza. We had all had it, but she was taking some time to get over hers and was more worried than ever.

As he was taking leave of me, in the corridor, he said:

"Would you mind coming around and having a look at my radio? I've an idea that one of the tubes has burned out."

It was dark by four o'clock in the afternoon and the street lamps were still painted blue, the shop windows unlighted. I had just finished a job when I remembered Dr. Wilhems, and I told myself that I had time to go over to his house before dinner.

I told my wife and put on my windbreaker. With my toolbox in one hand, I left the warmth of the house for the cold and the darkness of the street.

I had scarcely covered a few yards before a silhouette detached itself from the wall and came toward me while a voice called me by my name.

"Marcel."

I recognized her immediately. She was wearing a beret and a dark coat. Her face struck me as paler than ever. She fell in step beside me just as when I used to say to her:

"Come along."

She looked perished with cold, and nervous, while I remained calm and clearheaded.

"I've got to speak to you, Marcel. It's my last chance. I'm at Fumay with an English airman I'm taking to the unoccupied zone."

I turned around and thought I could see the figure of a man hiding in the Matrays' doorway.

"Somebody has given us away and the Gestapo's after us. We need to hide for a few days in a safe place until they've forgotten us."

She was getting out of breath as she walked along, something which didn't used to happen to her. There were rings under her eyes and her face was tired.

I was still striding along, and just as we were turning the corner onto the quay, I began:

"Listen…"

"I understand."

She always understood before I had opened my mouth. All the same, I wanted to say what I had to say:

"The Germans are watching me. Twice, they…"

"I understand, Marcel," she said again. "I don't hold it against you. Excuse me."

I didn't have time to stop her. She had turned back, running toward the man who was waiting in the dark.

I never mentioned it to anybody. When I had repaired the doctor's radio, I went back home where Jeanne was setting the table in the kitchen while Jean-François was already eating in his high chair.

"You haven't caught cold, have you?" she asked, looking at me.

Everything was in its usual place, the furniture, the various objects, just as we had left it all when we had left Fumay, and there was an extra child in the house.

A month later, I noticed a freshly printed poster on the wall of the town hall. There were five names on it, including an English name and that of Anna Kupfer. All five had been shot as spies, two days before, in the courtyard of Mézières prison.

I have never been back to La Rochelle. I shall never go back.

I have a wife, three children, a shop in the Rue du Château.

Noland, March 25, 1961

THE NEVERSINK LIBRARY

AFTER MIDNIGHT
by Irmgard Keun

978-1-935554-41-7
$15.00 / $17.00 CAN

THE ETERNAL PHILISTINE
by Ödön von Horvath

978-1-935554-47-9
$15.00 / $17.00 CAN

THE LATE LORD BYRON
by Doris Langley Moore

978-1-935554-48-6
$18.95 / $21.50 CAN

THE TRAIN
by Georges Simenon

978-1-935554-46-2
$14.00 / $16.00 CAN

**THE AUTOBIOGRAPHY
OF A SUPER-TRAMP**
by W. H. Davies

978-1-61219-022-8
$15.00 / $17.00 CAN

FAITHFUL RUSLAN
by Georgi Vladimov

978-1-935554-67-7
$15.00 / $17.00 CAN

THE PRESIDENT
by Georges Simenon

978-1-935554-62-2
$14.00 / $16.00 CAN

THE WAR WITH THE NEWTS
by Karel Čapek

978-1-61219-023-5
$15.00 / $17.00 CAN

AMBIGUOUS ADVENTURE
by Cheikh Hamidou Kane

978-1-61219-054-9
$15.00 / $17.00 CAN

THE DEVIL IN THE FLESH
by Raymond Radiguet

978-1-61219-056-3
$15.00 / $17.00 CAN

THE NEVERSINK LIBRARY

THE MADONNA OF THE SLEEPING CARS
by Maurice Dekobra

978-1-61219-058-7
$15.00 / $17.00 CAN

THE BOOK OF KHALID
by Ameen Rihani

978-1-61219-087-7
$15.00 / $17.00 CAN

YOUTH WITHOUT GOD
by Ödön von Horváth

978-1-61219-119-5
$15.00 / $15.00 CAN

THE TRAVELS AND SURPRISING ADVENTURES OF BARON MUNCHAUSEN
by Rudolf Erich Raspe

978-1-61219-123-2
$15.00 / $15.00 CAN

SNOWBALL'S CHANCE
by John Reed

978-1-61219-125-6
$15.00 / $15.00 CAN

FUTILITY
by William Gerhardie

978-1-61219-145-4
$15.00 / $15.00 CAN

THE REVERBERATOR
by Henry James

978-1-61219-156-0
$15.00 / $15.00 CAN

THE RIGHT WAY TO DO WRONG
by Harry Houdini

978-1-61219-166-9
$15.00 / $15.00 CAN